Fall On Me
Crossing the Continental Divide

Douglas Knick

www.ten16press.com - Waukesha, WI

For every father who has been blessed with a daughter or daughters. And to my daughters, Alexia and Anikka. When I close my eyes, I see you everywhere.

"A father holds his daughter's hand for a short while, but he holds her heart forever."

Prologue 1982

"I quit. Let's go home."

"It's a little late for that, wouldn't you say?"

"Then get this thing out of me!"

"First of all, it's not a thing, and second of all, you know that's not what we discussed."

"That was over four weeks ago. I am more than four weeks overdue. I think I can change my mind."

"Well, babe, we actually don't know you are four weeks overdue. The establishment of an actual due date is not a science unless, of course, we only had sex once a month, which you know wasn't the case."

"Keep it up, and it might just be once a year after this."

"What'd I say?" The look on his face confirmed that he was totally clueless at that moment.

"Oh my god, Gunter. Didn't they teach you anything about bedside manners in med school? You should demand a refund."

"I'm sorry, babe. Just focus on walking. One step in front of the other."

"Will you stop!" She stopped and stared directly at her husband. "I'm in here to deliver a baby, not to do physical therapy. Now shut up!"

Everyone on the hospital's second floor heard her words and knew she was serious.

The two ambled the remainder of the hallway in silence. Katharina cradled her belly with one arm and used the other to hang onto the

1

wall railing. Gunter awkwardly shuffled, partially at his wife's side and partially behind her. One look revealed that this was their first child.

Staring out the window at the end of the hall, Katharina and Gunter were startled when her assigned nurse approached them. "Mrs. Schaff, you need to return to your room. The doctor has ordered Pitocin. I need to start an IV."

"Pitocin?"

Gunter, without thinking, answered even though the question was directed toward the nurse. "Pitocin is used to stimulate contractions. It actually is meant to stimulate your natural oxytocin."

Raising her hand to her husband's face, she asked the nurse, "Does it have any effect on the baby?"

"We will start with a very low dosage, and if necessary, we can increase the amount if contractions don't start. As with any medication, there is always the possibility of side effects, but they are very rare, and we monitor the contractions closely once things start to progress. With Pitocin, your contractions tend to be stronger. The other option is to schedule a C-section."

Requesting her husband's assistance, she said, "Let's go back to the room so she can start the IV."

With the IV needle securely threaded into Katharina's vein, the nurse said, "The pole has wheels, Mrs. Schaff. If you wish to continue walking, you can. Just let us know the moment you experience any contractions or cramping."

"Don't worry. I'll let you know immediately if anything changes."

The next three hours were filled with walking the hall and returning to the room to rest. Her nurse wished Katharina good luck when her shift ended and introduced the nurse who would take over. The only change Katharina experienced was a throbbing headache, which she attributed to the stress of things not progressing.

At five minutes after five in the afternoon, things started to change. The labor pains intensified, as did the pain at the base of her neck.

With a firm grip on her hand, Gunter encouraged Katharina to breathe as they had practiced in Lamaze classes. The sound of air rushing across her lips filled the room.

As a contraction gripped Katharina, her complexion changed to a currant red, then to a blush as the muscles relaxed. Gunter dabbed her sweaty face with a damp, cool cloth and carefully fed her ice chips.

The small clock across from the bed read six thirty. Things should have been in full swing, but the pain associated with contractions ceased, while the pain in Katharina's head escalated. She wanted to scream as her head felt as if it was about to explode. Gunter no longer spoke. Noise, or any sound, seemed to penetrate her skull and increase the sharpness she felt. Katharina described the pain as a spike being driven deeper and deeper into her head while it felt as though her brain was expanding and pressing against her skull.

The drapes were pulled, and the lights were off to lessen any irritation to her eyes. Yet nothing brought relief.

Gunter sat motionless next to the bed, helpless, yet his mind raced to try to determine what might be unfolding and what was more serious at the moment, the contractions stopping or the pain building in his wife's head. What he knew for certain was that time was the critical factor in all of this. Some decisions had to be made, and made immediately.

Unfortunately, Katharina's doctor was down the hall attempting to save a cardiac patient, and ethically, Gunter couldn't offer any directive.

Unable to revive the patient down the hall, the doctor entered the room, exhausted and feeling defeated. His demeanor swung one hundred and eighty degrees as he monitored the baby's vitals. It was as though he shifted gears and was working in overdrive—competent, adept, erudite. He spoke first to the nurse and then to Gunter and Katharina. "Prep Mrs. Schaff for a caesarian section."

As the nurse left the room, he directed his words to the couple. "The baby is experiencing stress. Nothing to be alarmed about, but we need to take a different course of action. Once the baby has been delivered, we will address the headache. Are you both okay with this plan?"

Before Gunter could open his mouth, Katharina whispered, "Yes." She never opened her eyes or moved her head.

With a kiss that barely touched her lips, so as not to add any additional pressure to Katharina's head, Gunter watched as the medical team wheeled his wife into the OR. He knew the procedure that would unfold behind the closed doors. It would only be a matter of fifteen, at the most, twenty minutes, and their first child should be delivered.

The nurse appeared at the door of the OR with a bundle. Gunter noticed immediately that the nurse's cheeks were wet with tears. More than thirty minutes had elapsed since Katharina passed through the same doors. Placing the bundle in Gunter's arms, the nurse whispered, "I am so sorry."

"Sorry? Sorry for what?"

He looked down at his daughter, who wiggled her shoulders and yawned. The nurse disappeared back behind the door without providing clarity. He looked about the room for some help, but the waiting room was empty. It was just him and his daughter. Softly, he spoke to his daughter for the first time. "Sorry? Sorry for what? You have all your fingers and toes, and you squirm like a healthy infant who just left the warmth of her mother. Your mother?" The words hung heavy between his lips and his daughter's ear. He felt a twinge of guilt that the moment he saw his daughter, he forgot about Katharina. Stepping toward the OR door, he informed the precious cargo next to his chest of the purpose of his movement. "We need to get you back to your mommy."

Unable to gain entrance past the locked door, he awkwardly paced about the waiting room, bobbing his upper body forward and back, praying someone would emerge from the OR to invite him and his daughter to be reunited with Katharina, with Mommy. Being a physician increased his level of anxiety, for he knew this wasn't a proper procedure. Something wasn't right. Gunter read the doctor's body language when he passed through the door and knew that second that something was terribly wrong.

The nurse who followed the doctor into the waiting room took the infant from Gunter's arms as he was directed to have a seat. Before either could say a word, Gunter spoke. "I know the preamble you are to deliver. Just skip it and tell me what's wrong."

"Gunter," the doctor spoke as the nurse took a seat next to Gunter on the couch, holding his daughter as a mother would. "Katharina suffered a seizure of some sort. The moment the baby was delivered, her body began to shake uncontrollably, and she lost consciousness. We did ev—"

Tears streaming down his face, Gunter stopped the doctor. "She never saw or heard our daughter?"

"Honestly, Gunter, I can't answer that. I don't know."

For an unmeasurable amount of time, the three adults sat in silence and stared at the baby, who continued to stretch and yawn.

"Is she still in the OR?"

"Yes. I assumed you may want to say goodbye." The doctor spoke without removing his eyes from the baby.

Gunter had never really thought about the complexity of the phrase "goodbye" until that moment. Dismissing another with "good" seemed so strange in the face of death.

Gunter knew enough etymology to conclude that "goodbye" probably originated with "God's speed" or "God be with you." He wasn't sure what to think about God at that moment, so he stood and took his daughter in his arms. He informed both the doctor and the nurse, "I want Anya Katharina to feel her mother's body. She will never hear her mommy's voice or see the love in her eyes, but she will always have the feel of her mommy's body within her."

"Anya Katharina is her name?" Sobbing, the nurse was able to squeak out the question.

"Yes." Smiling in the face of tragedy, Gunter answered, "I don't have to argue with Katharina any longer about our baby's name. She didn't want the baby named after her. You see, Anya is her middle name."

Turning toward the OR door, Gunter lowered his head and spoke to his daughter. "Come on, Anya. Let's go see your mommy."

Summer 2019
Chapter 1

The asphalt, the width of the thoroughfare, and the rollercoaster-like design of the road, complete with whiplash curves and stomach-wrenching plunges, provided adequate evidence to query the wisdom of the posted speed limit. As if that wasn't enough, the multiple numbers printed on two different shadings caused angst.

"What's with the speed limit signs? Is this just a Montana thing?"

Gunter chuckled. "Boy, those take me back. When I started driving—"

"I didn't realize they had cars in the Stone Age." Her face wasn't visible, but it was clear from her delivery that she wore a smirk.

"Funny. Not!"

"Oh, Dad. That's so nineties."

"What do you expect from an old man? As I was trying to say, when I started driving, I believe every state had a speed limit for daylight and another for night driving."

"I thought eighty on the interstate was pushing the safety issue, but seventy on a two-lane highway?" Her words hung in the air as though she wasn't sure it was correct to refer to the blacktop as a highway.

"You needn't worry since it's dark. The speed limit is only sixty-five." The headlights from an approaching vehicle illuminated his face and the smile he proudly displayed as he delivered the words. He knew he was teasing her, and despite not having done so for countless years, it felt right at that moment. It took Gunter back to a time when teasing was the essence of how he attempted to comfort and soothe her whenever she was feeling overwhelmed or afraid.

From her room down the hall, a wailing sound disrupted the tranquil night. A night not unlike this one shrouded in darkness, concealing the beasts that waited at each curve or at the bottom of the hill. Waiting for the perfect moment to leap. It wasn't so much that teasing silenced the fear and doubts of a four-year-old, or even a ten-year-old, but that it kept him from admitting to his daughter that he, too, wrestled with the nightmares of fear and a sense of being overwhelmed. Sadly, despite the endless confessions, there always seemed to be a disconnect between what he wanted to do and what he did. He wanted to reach out and comfort his daughter, but his tongue was quicker than his arms.

"Holy shit." As the spit from his words stuck to the inside of the windshield, his foot slammed the brake pedal to the floor. "Did you see that?" If not for the seat belts, their chests would have been imprinted on the dashboard.

She pushed herself away from the dash. "See what?" Her voice wavered. "Between the mist, the wipers flapping back and forth, and the fog, I can't see anything."

The 2019 Chevy Traverse, with Gunter's foot still heavy on the brake pedal, idled quietly, pointing westward toward the town of Jordan on Route 87. Flexing his fingers to invite blood to return to the tips, he tried to explain what just happened. "Standing on the side of the road were two deer. It was as though they appeared out of nowhere. I-I was afraid they were going to jump out into the middle of the road." As an afterthought, he asked, "Are you okay?"

"I'm fine, more scared by your shouting than being tossed forward." As though contemplating the position of the car and how it wasn't moving, she asked, "I wonder how much rubber you left back there on the road."

The car pulled forward the moment Gunter released pressure on the brake, and he proceeded to offer context to justify his shouting and choice of words.

"Last fall I was driving home from work late in the afternoon. There was already snow on the ground; it was just a dusting, but it made the roads slippery. Anyway, I was the fourth vehicle in a string of five going roughly forty, forty-five miles an hour. Just as I was coming up on a large meadow, on the right side of the truck, a deer, a buck no less, leaped from the tall grass and onto the shoulder of the road. He navigated behind the rear fender of the car ahead of me but wasn't quick enough to clear the front end of the truck. Fortunately, and I say that tongue in cheek, the impact between animal and machine occurred at the very moment the deer vaulted in an effort to escape the entrapment between the car and the truck. As a result, after striking the left half of the front end of the truck, his momentum carried him across the road, rather than lifting him onto the hood and eventually into the front window."

"Dad! You never told me about the accident. Were you hurt?"

"No, I was fine. The truck, on the other hand, was not drivable. The grill was pushed into the radiator, so antifreeze was leaking out. The hood and left fender were crinkled, the bumper was severely dented, and, of course, plastic pieces littered the road. The damage totaled over six thousand dollars. Luckily, all I had to pay was the deductible."

"I'm glad it all worked out, but why didn't you tell me about the accident?"

"There wasn't anything you could do about it, so."

"So, you didn't think I needed to know."

"Yeah, something like that."

"Since we're on the topic of sharing things ..." Even though it was well past midnight and dark in the vehicle, other than the light shining from the speedometer and the radio clock, Anya positioned herself to face her father.

With his eyes firmly fixed on the road before him, he interrupted her. "I didn't realize we were on such a topic. Good heavens, we just passed five more deer all feeding in the ditch. They don't appear to be afraid of cars. This is so strange. There is no effort, at least from what I can see, to flee or to dart across the road."

Anya wanted to ask about her father's health and if there had been any more hospitalizations that he "forgot" to share with her. Feeling the pressure of the word *such*, she stopped herself. She knew there would be plenty of time during the upcoming week to have that conversation. The last ten hours had been some of the best time spent with her father. The conversation flowed freely, and she didn't want to threaten that by becoming impatient. She also realized the weight of her eyelids and that, at some point, he would ask her to drive, so she needed to sleep.

Pulling a blanket from the backseat and reclining her seat she asked, "Do you think it's safe to keep driving with the weather conditions and all the deer?"

"Yeah, I think so. Best I can tell, the deer are content to stay on the shoulder."

"I'm going to grab some sleep then. Wake me when you want me to drive."

Strangely, Gunter had to admit that he was thankful for the deer. He knew where Anya was headed with the conversation. It wasn't anything new. She wanted to know more about his life. It took the form of questions concerning his health, his work ethic, and his retirement plans, but the bottom line was that she was probing to learn who her father was. And that was a tough question to answer.

The search button controlling the radio, conveniently placed on the steering wheel, stopped at the one station that didn't fade in and out, regardless of whether they were at the bottom of a hill or circling a mountain. Gunter was glad that it was a country music station and not a station playing rap. Even better, it played classic country music, including the likes of Hank Williams, Buck Owens, Charley Pride, on and on. It helped pass the minutes between deer sightings and the wipers pushing the mist from the windshield. The DJ introduced the next selection by sharing the back story behind the song.

"Dolly Parton wrote the following song in 1973 and sang it to Porter Wagoner, her musical partner and mentor, in an effort to convince him that he needed to let her leave the band and strike out on her own. When Wagoner heard the song, he agreed it was time to go their separate ways. Dolly released the song a second time in 1982, and it again went to number one on the country charts." He then added, "This evening's recording is the original release. Sit back and let the music wash over you."

As though two lovers are seated next to one another, Dolly whispers the first few words, "*If I should stay,*" inviting the listener to share the intimate moment. The hint of hillbilly romanticism beneath Dolly's voice adds to the seduction and desire to hear more. The fullness of her voice swells the moment she speaks of love. "I will always love you." The inside of the car is transformed into "*Bittersweet memories.*"

Anya stirs and speaks over Dolly. "Dad, you didn't call the radio station and request that did you?"

"I swear, I didn't. It just came on."

With her shoulders raised off the seat, she squinted at the road before them and shook her head slightly before she shared her skepticism. "I find that hard to believe. Not with that song, Dad."

"You really think I'd call the station?"

"Yep! It's the original cut."

"You're right. It's the 1974 version, but you're still mistaken. The station plays classic country music. All the good stuff."

"Whatever you say," her tone dripped with sarcasm. She took a moment to center herself and avoid becoming a victim of the bottomless pit of frustration. When she spoke, her tone was sincere, "You need me to drive yet?"

"I'm okay. Go back to sleep."

"Even after that song, you're okay?" Anya became serious.

He took a moment before he responded. His tone was filled with sincerity and honesty. "Yeah, it's not like the old days."

With that, the two sat in silence and listened to the oldies streaming from the speakers. Anya drifted back to sleep, and Gunter permitted his thoughts to drift back to the first time he heard Dolly sing the final verse, "*But above all this, I wish you love.*" There was no way Gunter could have ever imagined how, just a few years later, that song, those words, would take on new meaning.

Chapter 2

After an hour's nap in the Walmart parking lot in Great Falls, Montana, Gunter woke Anya to let her know he needed to use the restroom. Surveying the parking lot, he joked, "If only I owned a motorhome like other senior citizens, I wouldn't have to walk across the blacktop in pouring down rain to take a leak."

Still half asleep, exhausted from driving the last three hours of the trek, Anya spoke to her pillow. "Dad, you know you will never own a motorhome. That would be too much luxury. We could wake up and not have a stiff neck and a stabbing pain in our back from the seat belt attachment. What fun would that be?"

"You going to stay, or do you need to pee too?" He considered responding to her crack about luxury. The issue wasn't luxury or the lack thereof; it was a matter of greed, selfishness, and frivolous use of resources, but the pressure from his bladder told him unless he wanted to wet himself, he needed to get moving.

"Are we pulling out when you return?"

"Yep. First things first, followed by locating a Starbucks. Then, down the road."

"Yeah, just give me a second. I need to pull myself together. You going to brush your teeth in the bathroom?"

"I already did."

Totally confused, she raised her head from the back seat and asked, "How? Where?

When?"

"Behind the car. I used bottled water to rinse."

"I'm surprised you didn't pee back there, too."

"I thought about it, but the camper next to us is a bit too close. Don't need an indecent exposure ticket."

"Glad you had second thoughts."

"I hate to end this conversation, but if I don't get to that bathroom, I am going to be wet where the rain doesn't reach."

"Go ahead. I'll meet you inside."

Four miles outside of Choteau, the Traverse turned left, leaving the state highway for Teton Canyon Road, a county road, and headed directly into the base of the mountains. Cruise control didn't need to be reset as the speed limit remained seventy despite the road narrowing by several feet. Eighteen miles later, the road turned to gravel, just as Dusty, the owner of the D Bar D Lodge and Outfitting Company, had warned. Another mile into the canyon again proved that Dusty's word was reliable, as the road became rough. More accurately, the road transformed into a trail that resembled a plowed field. The ruts looked like a black hole threatening to consume the entire vehicle. The final four miles before reaching the destination of D Bar D Lodge took longer to navigate than the previous eighteen miles.

Neither Anya nor Gunter spoke as the vehicle crawled forward. Anya was trying to envision what awaited their arrival while Gunter replayed the phone call that brought the two of them to this moment.

"Hey, Anya." Gunter owned a smartphone, not because he appreciated the technology and certainly not because he accepted the marketing pitch that such a phone made life easier; he owned a smartphone because Anya had purchased it for him as a Christmas gift. She knew her dad well enough to know that if he didn't recognize the phone number, he wouldn't answer and would simply wait for the voicemail if a message was left. She spent the better part of the afternoon, the day after Christmas, programming his phone with the names of people he identified as important. Although he would never admit it, she knew he liked the simple feature of caller ID.

"Hi, Dad. How are you?" To hear his daughter's voice brought a smile to his face. There were times, due to her schedule and his, that a month might elapse between phone calls.

"Yeah, I'm good. How have you been?" A phone conversation with Gunter could be challenging, unless it was related to medicine or horses. Most of his answers were short, and he usually deflected everything back to the person on the other end of the line. He loved to talk, just not on the telephone.

"As always, busy with work." Like her dad, Anya was driven by perfectionism when it came to her job. There was no forty-hour work week. The motivation wasn't to be the best, but rather to give one hundred percent for the sake of the other—something she witnessed Gunter do every day of his life.

As proud as he was of her academic and vocational achievements, he also was nervous about her working conditions. As a therapist, she specialized in working with adolescents. She was especially skilled at working with kids whose lives were filled with trauma. Unfortunately, at least from Gunter's perspective, her talent drove her to residential facilities, where she worked with kids who continually floated between the flight and fight mentality. His concern for her was compounded by the fact that he never verbalized that concern. He didn't want her to think that he doubted her abilities. And the truth was, he didn't doubt her; he just didn't trust the kids with whom she worked. His fears abated slightly when she started lifting weights, competitive weightlifting, and her five-foot-two-inch frame was transformed. Even though her philosophy would never permit her to use her physical strength to push kids around, it would, however, be useful when she needed to restrain an individual in fight mode.

He was quite sure he knew the answer. It had been discussed many times, but he asked nonetheless.

"Same old stuff or new issues?"

"Yeah, a bit of both. Frustration with staff and their inability or unwillingness to work with the kids rather than trying to always control them. I also have several new kids on my caseload, and it always takes time to develop that relationship where they trust me."

"New kids. Does that mean that some of your kids transitioned out of the facility?"

"Yeah, I don't think I told you the last time we talked. Three kids from my caseload left the home at the end of the school year. You can't imagine how that added to my stress level. Completing all the home visits and prep work required to prepare the kid and the family for their return home could easily have been a full-time job. That doesn't even take into consideration putting closure to those relationships."

"Which doesn't happen overnight. There's no switch to flip, no door to conveniently close that magically assists one in moving forward. I don't know about your graduate program, but I know there wasn't a course in med school that taught us how to do closure."

Anya wasn't sure which closure her dad was referring to—the death of her mother or all the patients over the years who, despite his efforts, still died. She wasn't about to inquire. That wasn't the purpose of the phone call.

"So, have you made vacation plans? It certainly sounds like you could use some time off."

"Well, Dad, that's partly the purpose of this phone call."

"Oh, yeah? Are you planning to come home?"

"Yes and no. After pulling a few strings, I was able to take off two full weeks."

"That's great. When?"

"The end of August."

"So how many days do I get to spend with my favorite girl?"

"What would you say to ten days?"

"Great."

"But you also have to take off ten days."

"Why?" It was as though the skepticism imprinted on his face was transported across the hundreds of miles that separated them from western Minnesota to Chicago. She knew well the wrinkles that formed on his forehead when he questioned something. As a kid, she was always relieved that his face wasn't frozen that way.

"Because I made plans for us."

"What kind of plans?"

"You remember how, when I was young, we would take a road trip every summer?" "Yeah, but what you probably don't remember is that most of those road trips were trips to medical conventions."

"You're right. I don't remember because all that mattered was that I was with my dad going to someplace other than Minnesota."

"Hey, there's nothing wrong with the Land of 10,000 Lakes."

"Not as long as you don't mind being carried away by mosquitos in the summer and fifty or sixty below windchills in the winter."

"So, I guess that means this plan of yours is for someplace other than Minnesota."

"I have booked a horseback trip into the Bob Marshall Wilderness. It's an eight-day trip, and I was thinking we could do an all-nighter, both driving out and back. What do you think?"

"Think? I'm not sure what to think." Gunter couldn't believe his ears. Ride horses for eight days in the wilderness of Montana? That was a dream come true, but riding a horse wasn't something that interested Anya, let alone enjoyed.

For years he tried to share his passion for horses and riding with Anya. He purchased horses of every color, horses that were slow and horses that were fast, horses that were bred to perform in the arena, horses that loved to chase cows, horses that rode best under an English saddle, and horses that carried a Western saddle. In the end, it didn't matter what horse he brought home for Anya; she just wasn't interested. Horses weren't her thing. And after a while, that, too, was okay. Therefore, his uncertainty was understandable.

"Come on, old man. You know you have always wanted to do a horse trip into the wilderness. You're not getting any younger."

"I have, and you're correct. I'm not getting any younger. But horseback riding? You really want to spend eight days riding a horse in the wilderness?"

"I know how this must sound, but yes, I really do want to do this. I think it will be fun to ride a horse in the wilderness with you."

"Fun may not be the word you will use after the second or third day. But it sounds like you have already booked the trip."

"I have, sort of. They are holding two spots because I knew you would need to clear your schedule. I told them I would let them know by tomorrow. I can send you the itinerary, and you can read about it. It's the end of August, and it's called the Continental Divide."

"I'll look at the itinerary, but I can give you my answer without reviewing the details.

Book it!"

"Thanks, Dad. I can hardly wait."

The wait was over as the vehicle crossed a narrow one-lane bridge that led directly to the D Bar D property. Gunter drove straight toward a corral as he missed the path that veered left and led to the lodge. As the SUV rolled to a stop, a middle-aged man pulled his foot from the bottom rail of the fence and made his way across a large green space.

Anya immediately spoke. "I bet that's Dusty."

Stiff from sitting and driving as they toured Glacier National Park before heading to the lodge, Gunter pulled himself from the vehicle and nearly tripped. Gunter thought to himself, *That was graceful. This guy, clearly a cowboy, must be wondering how I would survive a week on horseback.* Gunter used the fender to balance himself and make a better impression, as he met his host.

The man, with his cowboy hat set slightly to the left, spoke out of the right side of his mouth. "Hi, I'm Dusty." He extended his hand and waited for the visitor to state his name.

"I'm Gunter and this is Anya."

"Welcome to D Bar D Lodge. How was the drive?"

"Long."

"Where, again, are you from?"

"Minnesota. Anya's from Chicago."

"Two-day trip?"

"Actually, it's only sixteen hours. We left yesterday afternoon and pretty much drove straight through."

Dusty nodded, rubbed his chin twice, and then spoke. "You can head over to the lodge, probably, just back up to the driveway. Danelle is somewhere in the lodge; she'll get you set up in a cabin. Supper is usually at seven." With that, Dusty turned and headed back to the corral, where he was greeted by a buckskin, who parted the herd as he made his way to the fence.

The lodge was set on the other side of a creek, requiring visitors to cross a wooden walking bridge. The lodge, a log structure, looked like something out of a home decorating magazine. The wooden floor, the stone fireplace, the mounted prized animals strategically placed, the leather furniture, the family photos on the walls. Everything fit the stereotypical image of the Old West, including the hospitality. Danelle emerged through a narrow door from what appeared to be an over-sized kitchen. With her hand extended, she offered a genuine welcome and called one of the girls to escort Gunter and Anya to their cabin. Before Brit arrived, Danelle explained that they were welcome to make themselves comfortable in the large seating room, complete with the fireplace, if they liked. If a nap was in order, that was fine too. Supper would be ready by seven.

The afternoon air was damp and cool, as Brit, a twenty-something transplant to Montana, offered to help them unload their luggage and get settled in the cabin. The cabin, a mini version of the lodge, offered a stone fireplace, a bathroom complete with a shower, a spacious sitting area, and two bedrooms. The major difference between the two spaces was that anyone over the height of six foot two would need to duck at each rafter.

Before leaving, Brit said, "Feel free to turn the thermostat up to take the chill out or build a fire."

Anya, looking forward to the immediacy of heat and the desire to take a shower, located the thermostat and said they would save the fire for later in the night.

Waiting patiently for his turn to shower, Gunter relaxed next to the window with a glass of wine and absorbed the mountains that surrounded the lodge. Prayerfully, he acknowledged that God was indeed the greatest painter ever to exist. His canvas was earth itself.

Refreshed from a warm shower and filled with excitement for what adventures awaited them, they decided that rather than nap before supper, they would roam about the property. The first stop on the tour was a return to the corral, where Gunter pre-selected the horse he desired to ride. He realized he would not select the horse; that task was reserved for Dusty, but the act offered a topic for conversation as he and Anya stood at the corral and observed more than twenty-five head of horses and mules mill about. He could feel his daughter's nervousness as they surveyed the horses, and the hope was that time spent watching the graceful movement of these creatures would transfer a sense of tranquility and soothing peacefulness.

"I want to ride that one over there." With Gunter's arm extended and finger pointing, he directed their attention to the opposite end of the corral.

There was something about a black horse that captured Gunter's attention. Perhaps it started in fourth grade when his elementary class went to the library to select a book to read. As a fourth grader, Gunter's reading level was less than admirable. Struggling with dyslexia, reading a chapter book was nearly impossible. Both the librarian and the classroom teacher, Ms. Brown, tried to direct Gunter to the other end of the library that offered picture books and short stories. Their efforts were useless as Gunter would sneak back to the section of books directly beneath the clock on the wall that held Black Beauty on the second shelf, placed in the middle of the stack.

Although Gunter's horse, at the time, was a palomino, he wanted to add a black horse as a riding option. Every time Gunter proposed the topic, his grandpa would say, "What do you want another horse for? You can't ride two horses at once." That wasn't quite true. He remembered a time when he saw a woman place each foot on the back of two horses and ride them in a big arena while standing. But that wasn't why he wanted a black horse. He wanted to add to his adventures on horseback.

Each time he checked out *Black Beauty*, which occurred several times through the school year, the feel of the old book with its hard-cover and the smell attached to yellow pages blossomed upward and pulled him in. Seated quietly in the library, next to his classmates, pretending to read the words on the page, he created his own story filled with adventures as he rode Black Beauty.

"Let me guess," Anya said. "You want the black horse with the three white socks."

He stepped back from the corral and asked, "How'd you know?"

"How would I NOT know? Gee, Dad, *Black Beauty* by Anna Sewell. I can still quote most of the book. I think for three years straight, you read it to me every night."

"Oh yeah, I forgot about that."

"Seriously, you forgot? How could you forget the bedtime routine? I still can't go to sleep without reading several pages of a book. A book was one of the first things I packed for the trip. And, it couldn't be just any old book; it had to be a book that fit with the trip."

Smiling as though proud of his parenting skills, he asked, "So, what book did you bring to read?"

"*A Walk in the Woods*, by Bill Bryson."

"Is it any good?"

"I haven't started yet. I was saving it until we arrived here."

"Makes sense." Directing his attention back to the herd, he asked, "Which horse do you want to ride?"

She stood still for several minutes, looking over each horse. With her head adorned with a Minnesota Twins cap, she nodded toward a shorter, slightly petite, sorrel gelding that stood resting near the middle of the corral.

"Why that one?"

"Well, first off, he's standing near the middle of the pen, which suggests that he is comfortable and secure. Second, he is shorter, making it easier for me to get on and off. And third, he's got that glimmer in his eye that says he won't have any problems on the trail."

Gunter stood speechless. He never realized that she was paying attention all those years he was rambling on about horses.

After an extended period of silence, while they stood beside one another and watched the herd, Anya said, "Well, what do you think of my selection?"

Without removing his eyes from the herd, he answered, "Spot on. Spot on."

Looking at his watch, he suggested if they planned to see more of the property, they better get moving. Beyond their cabin, tucked beneath two massive trees that hid the roof of the building, sat another cabin. The entrance to the cabin faced away from the lodge and the other cabins, so when Gunter and Anya strolled by following a trail into the trees, they didn't notice that people were seated on the small porch, which had just enough room for two chairs.

"Heeey."

The word, delivered with a bass vibration, dropped from the sky as though God himself was speaking. The only problem with that conclusion was that neither of them thought of God as speaking with a southern drawl. Nonetheless, they were startled.

The gentlemen on the porch introduced themselves. The older of the two spoke first. "I'm Jack." Not the voice of God. The voice that drifted down from the heavens belonged to Bobby, who appeared to be a good ten years younger than Jack. Based on appearances, the two didn't appear to be blood relatives.

After a brief introduction by Gunter and Anya came the all-important question posed by Anya, "Where're you from?"

It was Jack who answered, "Athens, Georgia."

And Bobby provided the geographic description. "Which is located an hour northeast of Atlanta. Where are you from?"

"Chicago," Anya answered.

"Western Minnesota," Gunter added.

"Did you fly or drive?" Bobby leaned forward as he asked about their mode of transportation.

"We drove. From Minnesota, it's only about fifteen hours. How about you guys?"

"We flew. Arrived early this morning. Dusty came and picked us up along with another couple." Jack and Bobby seemed to have the discourse etiquette down as they took turns speaking without pausing to determine who would speak next. Jack continued to speak. "I guess there are just six of us on this trip."

"We were wondering how many were making the trip." Anya nodded toward her dad. "We were discussing the email from last week that referenced 'an interesting mix' of people who were making this trip. We wondered what interesting mix' meant."

Bobby looked at Jack as he spoke. "I was wondering the same thing."

Jack responded, "You suggesting that was directed toward me?" The two laughed. There obviously was more to their laughter than what appeared on the surface.

Leaning back against the wood rungs of the chair, Bobby asked, "Did you hear what time the evening meal is?"

"Yeah, Dusty said about seven o'clock."

Prior to the evening meal, Dusty, who stoked the fire with the assistance of Chuck, another guest, invited the six people making the trip, starting bright and early the next morning, to introduce themselves. Dusty nodded to Jack, who, it turned out, had made several trips with Dusty.

Jack, seated comfortably in a large rocking chair, which seemed to fit his style and manner, shared his passion for traveling the Bob Marshall Wilderness. When asked how many trips he had made with D Bar D, he struggled to provide a consistent response. He paused several times to think, and one could literally see him recalling the trips as his head nodded in sync with the movement of the rocker. After several attempts to count them, the best answer was that his first trip was in 2001. He remembered the year because of the events of 9/11.

Proceeding in a clockwise manner, Bobby described how he and his wife own and operate a horse and cattle supply store in Bishop, Georgia. Looking at Jack, he spoke of how Jack had invited him on previous trips, but it never fit his schedule. "This year, my wife said she could manage things at the store, and our daughter doesn't have any cutting events, so it worked to be here. As for horses, we have three cutting horses."

Hearing Bobby mention his three horses, Jack remembered that part of Dusty's instructions was to share if one has horses or done much riding. Jack interrupted, "Oh yeah, I forgot, I got a couple of horses and a couple of mules." Bobby just smiled as his friend spoke.

Dusty was next in the circle. He again welcomed the guests to the D Bar D and shared that he was looking forward to the next eight days. "There is some beautiful country to be seen and, if we're lucky, some wildlife." He paused for a moment before continuing. "Back at the ranch, we have roughly eighty head of horses and thirty-five mules."

"You still lead trips for elk hunting." Jack's rocker never broke the rhythm as he spoke.

"Oh yeah. After we finish up with this trip, we will head back to our first campsite to prepare things for the hunting trips."

"Are the elk numbers good? Didn't the fires take a toll on the elk in the Bob?" Jack's numerous trips into the wilderness of the Bob Marshall revealed firsthand the consequences of the wildfires. As a part of the circle of life in the wilderness, wildfires are not necessarily a bad thing.

"Yeah, well, it wasn't just the fires. The elk have been slowly decreasing in the mountains. The herds are pushing back into eastern Montana and western North and South Dakota. Elk are prairie animals that were forced into the mountains with western expansion, and now, they are slowly returning to their natural environment. I'll share a few more things about preparation for tomorrow, but let's finish with the introductions."

Gunter, wearing his tattered Stetson that had been reshaped countless times after being soaked in the rain, spoke briefly of the joys and challenges of being a doctor in rural Minnesota. He added, "I have wanted to do a trip like this for a long time, but it took my daughter here to make it a reality. I have six horses. Don't ask me why; I just do."

"You do because you have a soft place in your heart for horses." Anya smiled as she spoke, and Jack, Bobby, and Dusty nodded, knowing exactly what that was like.

Chuck sought clarity to understand why six horses. "You ride them all?"

With a nod, bringing the point of the Stetson nearly to his chest, Gunter said, "I sure do!"

Speaking out loud as his mind considered what that meant on a daily basis, Chuck continued, "That must keep you really busy."

"Sure does."

Chuck was preparing to continue his questions when Alice's hand lightly came to rest on his thigh, and he closed his mouth. Everyone, except for Gunter, turned to Anya. She read the nonverbal cue well and introduced herself.

"I was raised in rural Minnesota, but for the past twelve years I have lived in Chicago."

"Why Chicago?" The question came from Bobby, who also moved to a different state during his early adult years.

"I went to grad school in Chicago and landed my first job there and never left. I am an art therapist and currently work in a residential facility for pre-adolescent and adolescent kids. It's true. I suggested the trip."

"You have ridden all your life?" Dusty's question made perfect sense, considering Gunter.

"Actually, no. I haven't. I have ridden, but it never was my passion. Probably why Chicago works for me. Even though I suggested this trip, I gotta say, I'm a bit nervous."

With Alice's hand missing from Chuck's leg, he felt at liberty to respond. "You're not alone. I—" Before he could complete the thought, Alice's hand appeared directing him to stop talking.

In a comforting and fatherly manner, Dusty spoke directly to Anya, fully aware that others could benefit from hearing the same words. "There's nothing wrong with being a little bit nervous. I get nervous when people like you aren't a little bit nervous. It can result in a tragic outcome."

The words hung in the air for a moment, circling the trophy animals before Alice sat up straight and introduced herself. "I am Alice and reside in Philadelphia. Like Anya, after graduating from high school, I left the state in which I was raised. I have lived outside the United States and in several different states. I have had a variety of vocations. My current one is the most enjoyable as it aligns with my passion. I am a master gardener, and I work at a local nursery."

Chuck interrupted his wife. "Her previous job—" Alice's hand landed heavily, and Chuck didn't finish the commentary on Alice's vocational adventures.

"We don't own horses, and I never have. We do have a cat. Well, Chuck has a cat, which he shares with our son and daughter and me." Having finished the introduction, Alice slid back on the couch and waited for Chuck to speak.

"As Alice stated, we live in Philadelphia and moved there five years ago. I, too, have lived outside the United States. As an Air Force number cruncher, I was deployed overseas. We ended up registering for this trip at the last minute. Initially, we were exploring traveling to Vancouver. This year is a significant birthday for Alice, and so the itinerary was rather detailed. We planned to—"

The top of Alice's foot casually stroked Chuck's calf, which caused him to abruptly stop proceeding with his story. "Well, it doesn't matter. What does matter is that one evening, while discussing the plans for Vancouver, I remembered how my sister had been pestering us to take a horse trip with D Bar D. She and her husband took a trip five years ago and loved every minute. Ten years ago, we actually visited the lodge. My extended family was staying at Glacier National Park. It was my father's eightieth birthday celebration. During a day trip, we ended up here. My sister was so taken with the place they planned to return for a horse trip. The next morning at breakfast, Vancouver was out, and the horse trip was on. I have ridden a horse on a trail ride, but I have to admit, I am probably a whole lot more nervous than Anya."

Danelle, as though on cue, appeared in the doorway and announced that supper was ready. Dusty added, "We'll finish up after the meal to discuss tomorrow. Let's eat."

As Gunter turned off the light and retired to his bedroom, Anya, seated in front of the fire, said, "I'm feeling less nervous now. Thanks, Dad."

"I don't think I did anything, but you're welcome. See ya bright and early."

In the darkness of the bedroom, comfortably tucked under a hand-made stitched quilt, with horses in full stride, racing from the right edge to the left of the bed, Gunter pondered the origin of the phrase, "You're welcome." It bothered him that he so carelessly used words without knowing the full extent of their meaning. Fortunately, there was no internet access, or he would have been up half the night researching. It was difficult enough to get to sleep with the excitement of what awaited him and Anya at sunrise.

Chapter 3

The six of them patiently stood by the corral, with saddle horn bags in hand, and watched as the wranglers weighed, sorted, and grouped the luggage and eventually wrapped it all in canvas sheets in preparation for each bundle to be placed on the backs of mules. The conversation among the six noted the fluidity at which the wranglers worked in unison as well as venturing guesses about which horse they would be assigned to ride. Six horses also stood patiently outside the corral. The horses Dusty and the wranglers would mount stood saddled behind the tack room.

With the arrival of Danelle at the corral, the guests were invited to gather around one of the horses as she covered basic horsemanship. The short presentation started with Danelle directing everyone's attention to the sign that hung above the tack room. The words, carved into a rough chunk of wood, echoed across the uneven terrain of the valley to the point where the wranglers ceased their labors and looked at the sign as Danelle read aloud, "A horse is never wrong." To emphasize the importance of the credo, she spoke the words a second time, looking directly at the six guests. "A horse is never wrong."

Gunter smiled inwardly and wondered if Anya would appreciate the principle since she grew up hearing similar words, "A horse never lies." Gunter's explanation of those words was a bit lengthier than Danelle's. Gunter was fond of saying, "What a horse communicates is always the truth. Which also means that a horse is not stubborn. The issue is not the horse but people who are arrogant and refuse to listen and learn from the horse. Most people who claim a horse is stubborn are revealing their ignorance about how to communicate their desires to the horse and their inability to grasp what the horse is communicating."

Even though Anya knew that her father's words were true and his love for the horse was unquestionable, it still irritated her, like nails on a chalkboard, when words rolled effortlessly from his mouth. Therefore, she was surprised—shocked would be a better description—that he remained silent and didn't share his "witty" wisdom. As she stood listening to Danelle, she wondered if, with age, her father no longer needed to be right all the time.

Danelle concluded the horsemanship component with a positive reminder. "Your horse is a thinking, feeling creature. Be kind and don't ask him to do the impossible. He is your partner, not your slave. Treat him with respect, and he will take care of you. Alright, let's get you your horse."

One by one, the six were invited to come forward and meet the horse that would carry them into the wilderness and be their companion for the next eight days. Alice and Chuck were the first two to meet their horses. Alice climbed on a horse referred to as Letterman, which was previously owned by David Letterman, who owns a ranch in south central Montana. No one knew for sure if Letterman actually ever rode the gelding, but it made for an interesting introduction. Chuck cautiously mounted a stout, dark brown gelding. Bobby was handed the reins of a bay gelding with a black tail and mane. Dusty stood on the porch of the tack room and offered Bobby a pair of spurs.

"He moves pretty slow without a little encouragement." Bobby tied the horse to the hitching rail and thanked Dusty but said he had his own pair. Jack's horse was a sorrel gelding whose hips were massive and powerful. He immediately led the horse to a dip in the ground and stood on the small hillside to assist in mounting the tall horse.

Anya's horse, like Alice's, was more petite and not as tall as those the guys rode. The gelding, unlike the other horses, rode in a hackamore. She was thankful that Gunter always insisted that she ride with soft hands. It didn't take much to get her horse to stop. The last horse still tied to the railing was the black horse with white socks. Gunter just smiled as he strolled over, placed his boot in the stirrup, and swung his leg over the horse.

Confident that everyone's stirrups fit correctly, and after one last bathroom break, Dusty, ponying a mule, took the lead while the others fell in line as they headed out into the Bob Marshall Wilderness to ride the Continental Divide.

They had been warned by Dusty the night before that the horses would eat grass and that it didn't pay to fight with the horse. "You can keep them from eating, and at the end of eight days, they won't be testing you, but it's a short learning experience because the next rider will undo all the work you did and let the horse eat. So, it's just easier on everyone to let the horse grab a mouthful of grass every so often. Just don't let them stand and eat. If your horse starts to stop and eat, give him a little squeeze with your legs." It still caused a bit of frustration for those not accustomed to letting their horses eat endlessly on a trail ride.

The continuous rain the previous two days also made for interesting riding for the first couple of hours. The horses weren't skittish; they merely preferred to walk where there wasn't a foot of mud. Some riders let their horses navigate the selection of where to put their hooves, and others guided their horses to step where they perceived the footing was more solid and less slippery.

The first break, two hours into the wilderness, was a welcome relief for Chuck as his knees were killing him. Plus, Jack and Gunter needed to dispose of the fifth and sixth cups of coffee they drank at breakfast. The respite in a meadow also allowed the mule train, which left thirty minutes after the horses, a place to pass and go on ahead without having to do so on a narrow portion of the trail. The first two hours consisted of traveling through thick forest, on a narrow trail, and scaling a gradual grade.

The only sounds filling the trail the first hour away from the lodge were an occasional, "Oh, come on, you've eaten enough," or "Really? More grass?" which unexpectedly was followed by a horse forcefully expelling air through his nose to clear the tiny clover seeds that tickled the hair follicles. The sounds in the second hour, as the riders settled in and became comfortable with their horses, were conversations that filtered up and down the string of riders. They called attention to the breathtaking scenery that seemed to get more awesome with each clearing in the trees.

"The next two hours will offer a bit more of a challenge as the trail will narrow considerably, and we will be doing a number of switchbacks. Trust your horse. They know what they are doing. Once we make it through the pass, we will be on the back side of the mountain, and we will walk our horses for a while. We should get to our next stop about one o'clock, and we'll have lunch there." Those were the first words Dusty had spoken since he mounted his tank of a quarter horse and asked if everyone was ready for the journey that awaited them. They made an interesting pair, Dusty and his horse. The five-year gelding had no problem ponying the mule and permitted the mule from time to time to aimlessly bump into his hindquarters. Yet, if the mule attempted to get ahead or pull even with his shoulder, the gelding pinned his ears and tossed his head, informing the mule to back off. The horse's head seldom dropped in search of grass. He stood still whenever and wherever Dusty dismounted. But once Dusty's bottom touched the seat of the saddle, the gelding grew impatient. His head bobbed and he pranced in place. He literally was chomping at the bit.

The longer Dusty asked him to remain in place, the more exaggerated his actions grew. If it had not been for Dusty's patient demeanor, the gelding would have had reason to explode. His calming, consistent behavior offered the horse enough guidance and direction to express himself and remain within himself. Dusty modeled the words "Trust your horse," whether the group recognized it or not. He never drew attention to what he was doing or why he was doing it. He just did it and did it for the sake of the horse.

The break was extended longer than initially planned as the mule train didn't appear. Dusty explained how, on the first day out, the wranglers frequently needed to stop to adjust the loads or retie a pack or two. Everyone understood that in the middle of the wilderness, there wasn't any way to communicate with the wranglers. You trusted that everything was okay, and they would appear in due time. The previous evening, it was discussed that there was no cell service anywhere in the Bob and that Dusty, in the case of an emergency, had the ability to use satellite service to reach the lodge.

Again, modeling his trust for the wranglers and ability to adapt, Dusty said, "We'll move out, and they can pass us at lunch."

Gunter pulled in behind Anya and rode his black gelding, Monte, close behind in order to talk without having to shout back and forth. Even though Anya was thirty-eight years old, Gunter still thought of her as his little girl in need of protection. He purposefully directed

Monte ahead of Chuck that he might offer advice, if needed, once the trail conditions became more treacherous. He would have labeled his daughter as a novice rider. Confident and secure in a controlled environment but apprehensive and cautious in questionable conditions. Gunter would be among the first to say, "A dad is always a dad regardless of the age of the child."

When the trail moved above the tree line and the drop-off on the left side was several hundred feet, Gunter nudged his horse closer to Anya's and started talking. "Your grandpa would have loved to hike these trails. In fact, he probably did."

"Yeah, he was quite a boy scout, wasn't he?"

"As a scout leader, he may have even taken a boy scout group into the Bob Marshall Wilderness. I know he spent a significant amount of time in and around Glacier National Park."

"I wish I would have been able to spend more time with him. He was always so busy. It did enable Grandma and me to spend more time together, but still ..."

"Yeah, that was unfortunate. He was truly a Renaissance man. There wasn't a topic or a subject that he wasn't knowledgeable about. He could discuss any issue, and he could do so without making you feel inferior."

"Except for the topic of Mom."

"Mom?" Gunter jerked on the reins, stopping Monte on the trail. He didn't intend to stop the gelding; he was just surprised at how the conversation led to Katharina.

"Grandpa avoided talking about Mom. Whenever I asked about Mom as a child, he would quickly change the subject or send me off on an errand."

"Wow, I never knew that. I guess I never really asked him about your mom."

"You didn't need to. You had her right there."

Gunter couldn't answer. The hole in his stomach was aching. He never fathomed that talking about Martin, Katharina's dad, would lead to Katharina. Lifting the reins, Gunter slowed Monte's pace and created space between himself and Anya. He didn't want to avoid the topic, but he also wasn't prepared for what Anya might ask. The whole point of the conversation was to offer a distraction, not elevate the stress levels.

As they carefully slid past a boulder that jutted out into the trail, Gunter saw the first switchback, and his ears were filled with the roaring wind that swept through the pass high above them and rolled down the mountainside. Even if Anya wished to continue the conversation, it would have been impossible.

Riders tilted their heads to the right and leaned forward, narrowing the space between them and their horses' necks. At the first switchback, they quickly tilted to the left and then back to the right at the next switch. The bobbing of the head from side to side continued as they scaled the face of the mountain. Even the horses tucked their heads, pulling their noses close to the chest, in an effort to shield their eyes from the burning wind.

At one of the switchbacks, Gunter sneaked a peek at the riders on the ledge below him, and it reminded him of the bronze statue of a cowboy and horse entitled *Leaning into the Wind*. He was thankful that he had stopped at the tack room before they departed and asked one of the wranglers for a piece of string to tie his Stetson to his head. He would have been sad to lose his hat on the very first day.

In what seemed like an hour but was half that amount of time, the group reached the summit, and the raging wind blew directly in their faces until they reached the other side of the mountain and began their descent into the valley below. The trail on this side was twice as wide, and the footing was more stable. No rocks were threatening to give way beneath the weight of the horses, thereby casting horses and riders hundreds and hundreds of feet in a gorge. As a result, Dusty pulled back on the reins, stopping his horse, and invited anyone who wished to join him as he walked down the switchbacks. Four of the six riders dismounted and led their horses down the trail. With their lungs still struggling to recover from the wind, the group moved in silence. If anyone was inclined to speak, the words were delivered to their horse.

Lunch consisted of three pockets of riders finding a comfortable place to park their bottoms, which, for some, were growing numb. Two groups were comprised of two riders, and the third was a triad. Gunter and Anya asked if they might sit with Dusty. With a simple roll of his wrist, he invited them to join him and directed them to a seat on the log.

Finishing a mouthful of ham and cheese sandwich, Dusty asked Anya, "How's it going?"

"Alright. That wind and those switchbacks were scary at first. But then I realized the horse doesn't want to fall any more than I do, and that calmed my fears."

Washing his mouth with a swig of water, Dusty paused before speaking. "Yeah, that's part of knowing the horse is always right."

Without looking at Gunter, she offered him a comment. "Dad always said, 'Trust your horse.' I guess that's what I did."

The three of them finished lunch in silence and leaned back, resting in the tall grass until the mule train entered the meadow and passed on through with little more than a wave. When the trailing mule was no longer visible, Dusty announced, "We'll wait another fifteen minutes, and then we will head out. That will give them time to get the mules unloaded and start setting up camp."

A few minutes before three o'clock, the group rode into Round Creek Camp. The corral, where twelve mules and five horses from the mule train rolled from side to side on the ground to work out the kinks from the day, was as large and equally well constructed as the corral at the lodge. To the left of the corral were several hitching posts and a makeshift tack room covered with canvas to keep the tack dry. The camp also had a canvas-covered dining area and a kitchen complete with canvas walls to shield the space from wind, cold, and critters that rummaged the mountain floor in search of food. The luxuries of Round Creek Camp in the middle of the wilderness were impressive. The camp, for some expeditions, served as the base camp. Riders spent every night at the location. During elk season, the camp also served as the base camp. Each spring, Dusty and the wranglers carried everything in and set it up for the season, and then late in the fall, after the last hunt, with the trails packed with snow, they carried it all out on the backs of mules.

With the mules and horses free of saddles and bridles, it was their turn to carefully lower their large bodies to the ground and find relief from muscles that ached. The riders, whose footfall was considerably slower than eight hours earlier, wandered away from the corral in search of ways to soothe aching muscles. No one dropped and rolled, but as tents were put up, some of the six dropped onto an air mattress for a bit of shuteye. The rest of the group assembled on logs around the fire pit, minus the fire, and began the important work of storytelling.

The sun continued to perform its daily task of working toward the western horizon. With belt buckles slid one notch lower to provide space for bellies that expanded from the delicious meal, eleven bodies found a space to rest as Jack displayed his campfire-starting skills. The conversation of orientation, the rite of passage of discovering the perimeters of discourse, trotted forward, at times rough and uneven and at other times gracefully. They settled in. Everyone was given a voice, and a rhythm was established.

Inevitably, or unavoidably, there is that one individual who ignores the proper boundaries of etiquette and dives headlong into the shallow waters of taboo topics. The hairs on the back of the necks of a few campers stand on end, and others stare at the ground or deep into the flames to avoid eye contact. Ironically, the momentary uncomfortableness gives way to everyone taking a deep breath, and magically, they are willing to move beyond the shallow, safe discourse. The level of vulnerability increases, and authentic conversation emerges.

That was precisely what occurred the first night. The instigator came as no surprise to the other ten, whose shadows climbed the base of the trees that engulfed the firepit. Chuck, who took to standing slightly outside the circle, cast a dominating shadow into the trees as he probed the stories that were offered up to the fire as a sacrifice. It was sincere in that the questions were for clarification and his own understanding, yet it laid outside the boundaries of proper campfire conversation. Beyond the reach of Alice's hand, there was no one to filter his queries which frequently disrupted the flow of the story being told. And when Chuck offered up a story, the message became lost in the details, and yet, a bond emerged as nearly everyone sat patiently, accepting Chuck for his uniqueness. The exception was Alice. She nervously rocked on the log, wishing her husband was within arm's reach.

As the stories waned, Anya was the first to call it a night and left the warmth of the fire for her sleeping bag. Gunter pulled the flap open twenty minutes later and found Anya reading by the light of a headlamp. Both agreed before the trip that they would read something related to wildness, horses, or camping. Anya selected *A Walk in the Woods: Rediscovering America on the Appalachian Trail*, by Bill Bryson, and Gunter brought *Out of the Wild*, by Mark Rashid. Gunter's book selection fit the environment par excellence. His excitement for the book was rooted in the fact that he knew Mark and respected him both as an author and horseman. He had only allowed himself to read the opening pages of the book, but now he could cradle the book in his hands and be drawn into another story carefully crafted by Mark Rashid.

His headlamp cast a brilliant white glow on the pages when Anya's voice interrupted Gunter. He was busy creating a mental picture of Henry, a central character of the book. Gunter didn't mind conversing with his daughter, but seriously, couldn't she see he was reading?

As a young child, Anya had been taught that there were times when Dad needed silence, moments of not being interrupted so that he could read materials related to his work. As a single parent, Gunter tried to be home as much as possible, which meant bringing home medical records to complete, files to prep for the following day, and medical journals to stay fresh and current on the latest research. Surely, she hadn't forgotten; he didn't appreciate her interruption.

Without moving the light from the pages of the book, Gunter asked, "What'd you say?"

"I asked, whatever happened between you and Susan?"

"Susan?" The treasured book fell to his chest, and his head rolled to the left to make eye contact with Anya. Was she serious? Susan?

Blinded by the headlamp, Anya shouted, "Dad, your light."

He fumbled for the tiny button as he offered an apology. "Sorry."

With the light still projecting her profile on the canvas of the tent, Anya continued, "Yeah, I have always wondered what happened. It was as though she just disappeared from our lives."

"Susan," speaking to himself, having located the button. "Now there's a name I haven't heard for a long time."

"Dad!" Anya's voice was just an octave below a shirk. "She's more than a name."

"Yeah, yeah. You know what I mean."

"Actually, I don't know what you mean. Just like I don't know what happened."

A puff of air whiffed from somewhere deep within Gunter. The air carried multiple levels of meaning. *Do we really have to visit this topic now? Why would I want to revisit my relationship with Susan after so many years? What is Anya really up to, and where is this all leading?*

She read the silence on her father's part as he scrolled through a litany of questions. In her mind, she thought, *God, how I remember his endless list of questions, and in the midst of the barrage lay the true motive, avoidance.* She also acknowledged to herself that over the years, she became skilled at concealing her objective, and only after days, weeks, or even months later would she bring it full circle.

It started, in all honesty, at the tender age of three and a half.

"Daddy, why does the moon shine?"

"Well, it merely reflects the light from the sun."

"But the sun doesn't shine in the night."

"Not where we are living, but on the other side of the earth it shines when it is night here. The light from the sun strikes the moon, and that's what we see."

"Daddy, why do we read *Good Night Moon* every night when the moon doesn't go to sleep?"

"It's only a story, honey, and in stories you can do things that don't really exist."

"But dollies exist, and they're in the book."

"Yes, dolls exist."

"Do dollies come in different colors?"

"Yes."

"I only have white dollies."

"That's because you're white, and that's what your grandparents bought for you."

"If I was Black, I'd have Black dollies."

"Yes."

"Daddy, why?"

The questions went on until Gunter stopped answering and finished *Good Night Moon*. Two weeks later, when they were at the store, Anya said, "Daddy, buy me a Black dolly."

"Why do you want a Black dolly?" The conversation about dolls never registered. "Samantha doesn't have a Black dolly. She needs one."

"Let her parents buy her one."

"She doesn't have a daddy, and her mommy said they don't have the money. You buy it."

The questions in Gunter's mind while he stared at the tent pitch continued accumulating. *What is she really up to here? What is she truly asking? Is this really about Susan, the woman she knew for three years, from the age of six to eight? Good heavens, that's more than thirty years ago.* Finally, he just had to ask. "Anya, Susan hasn't been in our lives for more than thirty years. Why are you asking this now? What brought that name forth?"

"Do I need a reason?" Typical Dad. Always questions motive. Always guarded. Never just rolling with it. Avoiding answering a question for fear he might make himself too vulnerable. He might accidentally show a true feeling, a feeling he's tried to bury, a feeling that might make him appear weak.

"No, of course, you don't need a reason. I'm just thinking, here we are, in the middle of nowhere, and you are asking about Susan. Seems strange, doesn't it?"

"Why not try answering the question rather than trying to determine my intentions." "Because there is generally always some hidden agenda attached to your questions." "That's not fair." Anya no longer attempted to lower her voice.

"It's not? You honestly can say there's no ulterior motive at work?"

"Dad, you're only stalling."

"And you're only avoiding."

Silence filled the space around them. In the game of chess, which they both love to play, this could be labeled a stalemate. However, for totally different reasons, neither was willing to acknowledge that a stalemate was possible.

Gunter made the first move. "Why not just drop the question for now?"

"Why not just answer it? It's not that difficult."

"Who gets to decide what is difficult? You?"

"STOP!"

There was no doubt that the entire camp heard Anya shout, including the livestock that drifted up the mountain in search of grass. Gunter could only wonder what the others were thinking.

"Anya, quiet down. There is no need to shout."

"Right, Dad. Never show your emotions."

"Oh, god, not this again." It was Gunter's voice that now moved the flap of the tent. "What, again?"

Tired of the conversation and afraid of where things were headed, Gunter addressed the question. "Susan." He stopped momentarily, recognizing that he had forgotten the actual question. "What was it again you asked about her?"

Calmly, Anya spoke, "I asked, whatever happened between you

and Susan?"

His head rolled back to the center of the makeshift pillow, which was a hooded sweatshirt stuffed inside a small, soft commercial bag. Carefully, he removed his book from his chest. He took a second deep, cleansing breath and spoke into the pitch of the tent. "The short answer is she wanted more than I was willing to give. She wanted to get married. She wanted to be Mrs. Schaff."

"Did you love her?"

"Yeah," he paused for a moment, "I suppose I did."

"What the hell does that mean? You suppose you did?"

"She wasn't your mom."

"Of course, she wasn't. No one is Mom, but Mom wasn't Susan either."

His head cranked left. He had never heard her speak such things about her mom. "What the hell does that mean?"

"It means Susan had gifts Mom didn't."

An edge of anger spit from his mouth as he responded. "You can't say that. You never knew her." The moment he said it, he regretted the words. It was just plain stupid.

"Thanks for reminding me. I nearly forgot."

"Anya." He stopped himself. He was sorry, but to actually say it was too dangerous. He might totally fall apart. He tried to remember if Anya ever saw him cry. It wasn't that he was embarrassed to cry; he just wanted to protect her. Secretly, which he seldom allowed himself to consider, he was also trying to protect himself.

At the time of Katharina's death, he cried to the point that his tear ducts went dry like a mountain creek in August. He eventually realized that he reached a point where he used crying as a means to avoid moving on. If it hadn't been for Anya, that tiny baby who simply wanted and needed someone to feed her, change her diapers, and above all

44

else, love her, he probably would not have survived the ordeal.

The baby became the process of healing. With a screaming baby, there wasn't time to feel sorry for himself or vegetate in the absence of Katharina. There were still moments and places that stopped him in his tracks, moments and places that startled him like an unexpected balloon popping, but he learned how to avoid those places and moments. Katharina's closet was just one such place.

The day Gunter and Anya arrived home from the hospital, he conveniently avoided Katharina's closet. It was Kat's mom—Gunter never could get used to hearing Katharina called anything but her given name, unless it was the pet name Babe he had given her—who first experienced his method of dealing with his wife's death. She was in the master bed with Katharina's closet doors wide open. She was pushing hangers and clothes from one end to the other when Gunter stepped in from the hallway with Anya in his arms. Seeing the doors open and his mother-in-law touching Katharina's personal effects, he nearly dropped his daughter.

Trying not to explode, he labored to utter the words as slowly as possible, and they still came forth quickly. "Hildy, what are you doing?"

Startled to learn she was no longer alone in the house, she stuttered a reply. "I, I—I'm loo-lookin' for a d-d-dress for the funeral."

"Thank you." As politely as possible, he spoke with Anya pressed against his chest. "I decided that rather than search for a dress, you know how Katharina could stand for hours searching for just the right dress, we would buy a new one."

With the hot flash of fear subsiding, she spoke calmly. "I think that's a great idea. I started going through these clothes and sorting them into piles." Hildy didn't immediately grasp the full weight of her son-in-law's suggestion.

Gunter couldn't believe what he was hearing. Katharina's own mother rushed to get rid of any sign of her own daughter. Harnessing all the energy imaginable from within, he carefully chose his words. "Hildy, I don't want to sound ungrateful, but isn't it too soon to start going through Katharina's things?"

Backing out of the closet, Hildy realized that her way of dealing with her daughter's death was to keep busy, and Gunter's way was to avoid any reminders of Kat.

"You're right. I am so sorry. Tell me what you need me to do."

In the tent's darkness, Gunter absorbed the moment and softly nodded as he acknowledged that Anya inherited from her mom and her grandma, the Martha Complex. It was more than busyness, which Martha is attributed with, as her sister, Mary, sits at the feet of Jesus. It encompasses a keen astuteness of the needs of others and a willingness to advocate for others as well as for themselves. It was one of the many facets of Katharina's personhood that Gunter simultaneously admired and found challenging. Anya displayed the same personhood, the same determination from the moment she took her first breath so that, while Gunter rejoiced in her strength and tenacity, it frequently overwhelmed him, leaving him shaking his head.

Anya had every right to ask about Susan. What was the source of his fear? *Oh, Katharina. If only, if only.* Gunter couldn't begin to count the number of times he prayed those very words over the past thirty-eight years. It wasn't fair that Anya should have to live her life without a mother.

The only thing he could say was, "I am sorry." It was barely a whisper. The weight of the words was so heavy that they pressed upon his throat. The words represented an apology covering an entire lifetime. It was only three words, and it was whispered, yet it was a start.

Chapter 4

Gunter's dreams were teeming with visions of Susan, which led to a restless night of sleep—if one could even call it sleep. Using the excuse that he needed to relieve the pressure in his bladder, he left the tent before sunrise while Anya was still sound asleep.

With a cup of steaming coffee, Gunter dragged a chair a short distance from the table to the wood stove in the dining hall as Shatz, a wrangler and Dusty's daughter, busied herself with making breakfast. With the flaps of the canvas lowered to keep the cold from luring the heat from the stove outdoors, Gunter warmed his left side as his thoughts swirled with images of Susan. He hadn't thought about her since the day she walked out of their life. She had been the first woman he permitted to get emotionally close to him since Katharina's death.

Susan Freund, an RN, arrived at the medical center fresh out of college and only days after she had passed her state boards, which, as she said, allowed her to make real money. At the age of twenty-three, Gunter was Susan's senior by ten years. A simple fact that caused Gunter considerable difficulty as their relationship developed over time.

It wasn't love at first sight. In fact, Susan didn't perceive Gunter as an eligible widower, only as Dr. Schaff. Gunter's initial reaction to Susan's presence in the medical center was, "She seems a bit overly confident, for being a newly licensed nurse, and so young. Sometimes it is better to watch and learn before offering advice on how to perform a task better."

Beyond the scope of work, the two didn't socialize. Any conversation was prompted by a change in a patient's condition. The annual Christmas party changed that. It was an event Gunter attended only because he was pressured into making an appearance. Fellow physicians informed Gunter that if he didn't want to be identified as a snob, he needed to attend. His response was, "I'm not a snob; I have a six-year-old at home who needs me."

In unison, he heard, "For one night, she'll survive with a babysitter. She might even enjoy a break from you."

Grabbing the punch bowl ladle, Gunter's hand covered Susan's. They both had reached for the ladle at the same time. He laughed nervously while quickly pulling his hand back as if he were stung by a wasp, and she said, "I was here first." He agreed, and she offered to fill his cup with spiked punch. Drifting away from the punch bowl, she confessed that she hated such gatherings.

Half of those in attendance didn't want to be there, and the other half were getting drunk on the medical center's dime.

Surprised by her candor, Gunter stopped and watched her take another three steps before she noticed he was no longer at her side. She turned and looked back, wondering what happened. As he stepped forward, he smiled and said, "I thought I was the only person who thought that."

"You don't enjoy these events, either?" Susan appeared startled by the thought that Dr. Schaff wasn't enjoying himself.

"Heavens no. Honestly, this is the first one I ever attended." The crowd shifted to the right, and Susan was shoved into his chest. First, he smelled her. Second, he felt her feminine curves against his body, and then, he realized his face was flush with embarrassment.

She found a minute amount of space behind her and stepped back to look into his eyes as she spoke. "So, what are we doing here?"

He shrugged his shoulders and asked, "You want to go and get a cup of coffee or maybe a real drink?" He held up his cup as those mocking the beverage.

"Coffee's good; a real drink is better. Do you know where we can get such a thing?"

He leaned in a bit closer to ensure she could hear him over the band and to steal a second whiff of her perfume. "I know of two places. The first one is a small hole in the wall. The bartender doesn't cheat on the liquor, the prices are from the 1960s, and it's fairly quiet. Unfortunately, the selection of drinks is limited, nothing fancy or sweet."

"You mean, no little umbrella in the drink?"

"No umbrella, no little spears, and we'll be the topic of conversation in the café tomorrow morning. The second place has a more extensive selection of drinks, including quality liquor. The prices are high, and the place will be crowded with holiday parties, but we will blend in and go totally unnoticed. So, what's your choice?"

She crossed her arms beneath her ample breasts and thought for a moment before an intoxicated anesthetist bumped into her, driving her into Gunter's arms. Pushing herself away from his body for a second time, she asked, "Is it possible to do both?"

Gunter, again, was shocked by her response. He found himself enjoying the unpredictable comments of this woman, despite her age, or maybe because of her age. "I don't see any reason why not. Preference where we start?"

"Yeah," she smiled as though suggesting there was a hidden meaning to her words. "Let's start with the noisy place and end with the quiet place. Who knows—" She never finished the sentence.

Jack, the other caffeine junky, pulled back the canvas flap and slid his body through the opening. "Coffee done?"

Before Gunter could answer, Shatz shouted from the other end of the hall, "Oh yeah, brewed a while back. Just simmering for you."

"Good and strong, like I like it?"

"Yep, just for you, Jack. Just for you."

Jack dragged a chair toward the stove after having opened the grate and carefully placed another log in the belly of the stove, and Gunter knew his journey back in time to meet Susan was put on hold. Jack loved to talk. Gunter didn't mind because Jack had a way of making the ordinary extraordinary, the obvious original, and the boring engaging.

Within minutes, Gunter was laughing so hard that tears rolled down his cheeks. The salty droplets mingled with the stubble of the beginning of a beard.

"Cramps kept me awake half the night. I took my pill, even popped a second, before I crawled into the sleeping bag, but it didn't stop the cramps. It was thirty minutes later, and I was wailing in pain. Cramps. Can't stop them once they start. Bobby even tried to rub them out, but it didn't help. I was pretty loud; did you hear me? Those damn cramps."

Gunter hadn't heard a thing, but he couldn't help himself. "Yeah, Anya and I were wondering what that howling sound was. It sounded like a sick, dying coyote."

"I had them again this morning, an hour ago. My legs started aching and, sure enough, cramps. First the right and then the left, both legs at once. That's just not fair. Bobby woke up and started laughing, and wouldn't you know it, he got cramps. Right leg. We were both laughing and moaning at the same time."

"I heard that too."

"You did, ha? I thought we kept it down. I know last night was loud, but this morning, too, huh?"

"Yep."

Fifteen minutes later, Bobby slipped through the canvas flap, filled his mug with coffee, and dropped a chair next to the stove. Gunter couldn't resist. "That was quite the noise bellowing from your tent last night and this morning. I thought there was a coyote dying somewhere."

"You heard that?"

"Sure did. Sounded something awful."

"It was awful, cramps in our legs. First, Jack and then me." Then, as though speaking to himself, his head shook, and he finished with a whisper, "You heard that, huh?"

Gunter considered, for a split second, confessing that he didn't hear a thing, but before he could speak, Jack was telling Shatz about his cramps and then Bobby's. To confess might ruin the mystic surrounding "the cramps."

The three of them, working on a second cup of joe, stopped their conversation when the ringing of cowbells infiltrated the tent. It sounded as though the herd was about to storm the dining hall. It was amazing how the sound, any sound, echoed endlessly.

Checking her watch, Shatz commented, "The herd must have been way back in the canyon. Usually, Quad has the horses and mules back long before six-forty. It doesn't matter. Breakfast isn't until eight."

Dusty initiated the conversation following breakfast. "What would everyone like to do today? We can do a short-day trip on horseback."

"My knee is pretty sore. I doubt I want to climb back on a horse to-day." Alice had been the first to take a nap after yesterday's ride and the last to arrive for breakfast. Chuck had shared that she was struggling both with a headache and an endless ache in her right knee.

"There's also an easy hike up Wapiti Ridge. It's not that strenuous. Might be just the thing your knee needs to stretch it out." Dusty stared at the mountain as he spoke.

"How long of a hike is it?" Anya asked.

"Well, it is probably a mile, maybe a mile and a half. Nothing too steep. And, of course, one doesn't have to do anything."

Jack was the first to decline the offer to go hiking. "I'll do the trail ride."

Bobby agreed that the trail ride sounded more inviting. Chuck and Alice discussed the options at length, with Alice thinking the walk might do her some good. Chuck agreed that he wasn't ready to place his butt back in the saddle. Seeking more clarification about the hike, Chuck asked, "Where is this Wapiti Ridge? Is that what you called it, a ridge?"

Shatz pointed to a mountain peak off in the distance and added, "I have taken many groups on the hike. It's not bad, and once you get to the top, the view is spectacular."

Seeing how far the peak looked from camp, Chuck turned to Alice and asked, "You think you can handle that distance?"

Alice shook her head and said, "I think I will stay here and rest my leg and start the book I brought along. You go ahead."

"You sure you don't mind if I go? Because I sure don't mind staying here with you."

"No, I would prefer that you went. It will be quieter here."

At the last minute, Anya and Gunter decided that they would join the hike as well.

Neither realized that the other joined with the hope of walking off some frustration. The source of the frustration was different for each of them, yet both were feeling the rise of their emotional barometer.

It was determined that those riding and those hiking would leave for their expedition at ten o'clock. The policy was when guests left the camp for an extended journey, a wrangler would accompany them. The wranglers decided that Dillon and Brit would hike, Dusty and Quad would saddle up and ride, and Shatz would stay in camp since Alice elected to stay back.

As the wranglers discussed who would go where, Shatz was the first to speak. "I have climbed Wapiti countless times. I'll stay back. I have some studying to do anyway."

Shatz, like her dad, was not your typical college graduate. It probably started with her name, Shatz. She had been named after her great-grandma, Charlotte, who bore the nickname Shatz. Her great-grandma had received the name from her sisters, who, in their effort to pronounce Charlotte, ended up saying Shatz. The name stuck, but she was a lot more than a nickname. Moving West to follow her true love, she ended up in Choteau, Montana. She left her mark throughout the town, having owned and operated the first movie theater, supported the efforts of other businesses, toiled with her husband to develop a thriving cattle operation, and most importantly, raised a family.

The birth certificate says Charlotte, but from the moment Dusty cradled his firstborn, she bore the nickname Shatz. She wasn't your typical wrangler in that her way with both horse and mule was soft and gentle. Her voice was never raised, her movements were slow and precise, and four- and two-legged mammals respected her. In May, she graduated from college, and whenever she had a few minutes free, she was studying for her nursing boards.

After everyone had crawled into their tents at night, she sat next to a lamp pouring through her notes. In addition to assisting with loading the mules, she could wrap a pack as fast as any, and she also served as the cook. Her creativity with the meals, considering what she had to work with, was welcomed by wranglers and guests. Like her great-grandma, there's no doubt, she would leave her mark.

Shatz's explanation of her name around the campfire the night before was not lost on Anya. She could appreciate and comprehend the full extent of the joy and the burden of being named after someone whom you never met. Someone whom you came to know through the stories told by others. Stories to inform you that you bear the name of someone special. Anya could feel the elation and the weight of being connected to someone from the past, yet she held her tongue.

Dillon, an eighteen-year-old Eagle Scout, took the lead, and the other four fell in line. They were accompanied by Ava, a four-year-old dog that Brit adopted during her brief stay in Arizona. She was fond of saying Ava was the best thing to come out of Arizona. After a fifteen-minute climb out of Round Creek Camp, the group emerged from the tree-covered trail and was greeted by a large meadow that provided nourishment for the herd during the night, as witnessed by the droppings.

Stopping to let the group catch up, Dillon chewed on the end of a long-stem weed. As the four winded hikers arrived, Dillon confessed, "I have never done this hike, but it shouldn't be too challenging." Pointing across the meadow, he continued, "That's where we're headed." With that, he turned and set off while Anya and Brit were sucking down water.

The march across the meadow was less strenuous, even though there was no marked trail. The chatter among the four was nonstop. At times, four different conversations were going at once, and they went in four different directions. Only Dillon avoided the messiness of the chatter as he was too far ahead to hear their words.

The tension that resulted in Gunter and Anya selecting the hike wasn't noticeable. The two had lived under the umbrella of unspoken tension for the better part of Anya's adolescent years so that they became skilled at concealing it from others, occasionally from each other, and periodically from themselves. The tension, at times, had been so thick that if asked, neither of them could name the source. Neither could identify what frustrated them the most. Neither had the strength to move. It was as though they were stuck in freshly poured cement, and it was hardening quickly. It was only Ava who sensed the strain that leaked from their pores mingled with sweat. As a result, she forced her head under their hand, bringing forth a pet or two before she was off racing to get ahead of Dillon.

Forty-five minutes into the thick of the wilderness, including climbing over and under fallen trees, wading through dense brush that refused to yield to thighs while maintaining balance as the terrain was a continued rollercoaster, the word *bushwhacking* emerged. Initially, it was little more than a whisper, which eventually developed into a complete sentence. Chuck was the first to say, "Well, at least I can say I have been bushwhacking." Finally, with a play on words, and no longer attempting to conceal exhaustion mixed with frustration, the forest was filled with, "I think we have been bushwhacked!"

Gunter didn't mind the trek through the wooded jungle. He carefully watched Dillon, the young Eagle Scout, carve small notches on the trunks of trees with his pocketknife and break branches to serve as signposts for their return trip. Gunter realized Dillon didn't know exactly where he was headed and that the hour-and-a-half trip, already more than an hour old, would be more than twice as long. The labor of pushing through the dense growth was demanding, but that brought silence to the hikers as they needed to conserve their energy. The silence afforded Gunter the opportunity to invite Susan back into his thoughts, and for that, he was thankful.

Monday morning, the medical center was abuzz with the gossip that Dr. Schaff and Ms. Freund were seen together at the Hole-N-Wall bar Saturday evening after the Christmas party. The gossip didn't bother him. The pat on the back from fellow doctors he could ignore, the coy smiles from other employees he could dismiss, but what concerned him was that somehow Anya would learn of the night out with a woman and conclude it was a date.

The "who knows?" evening ended with Gunter driving Susan back to her apartment and attempting to shake her hand in appreciation for a nice evening, only to have her lips plastered against his. He didn't pull back, but he also didn't kiss back. As Susan stepped back and opened her eyes, she said, "I guess that means you're not coming in."

Without a moment's hesitation, he answered, shaking his head, "No, no, I can't. It's not you; it's just that I can't. I have a litt—"

She stepped closer, kissed his cheek, and said, "I understand. You don't need to explain."

For the third time that evening, Susan surprised Gunter. Adhering to the rule of three as being something special, Gunter realized at that moment that he needed to get to know this woman.

With the start of a new year, Gunter decided that it was time to learn more about this woman who surprised him. It had been nearly a month since the Christmas party, and the gossip at the medical center had moved well past Gunter and Susan and the Hole-N-Wall bar.

However, Gunter decided that rather than add fodder to the gossip mill by going out in public, he would invite Susan over to the house for dinner. That way it wouldn't be misconstrued as a date, and he could justify to Anya why he invited a woman to have dinner with them. He would play to his daughter's social conscience. Susan lived alone and, therefore, ate her meals alone, and no one likes to eat alone. Gunter proposed that they make the meal together and share it with Susan.

It didn't take six-year-old Anya but a second to jump at the chance to cook and share the fixings with another person, especially a woman.

The meals became a monthly gathering with Anya as the chef and then a weekly event. Before the calendar had been flipped six times, the three of them sat down for an evening meal nearly every night. The gossipers at the medical center didn't have much to chew on since Anya was always present. Susan left the house for her apartment shortly after Anya recited her bedtime prayers and fell asleep under the glow of a nightlight.

Susan was the first to declare her love for Gunter. He remembered the night well. It was Thanksgiving. Both their parents had departed for home, and Anya was asleep. Gunter's hands were deep in the sink, scrubbing the turkey roaster, as Susan had just finished drying the platter that had held the turkey. She carefully draped the damp towel over her arm and pressed her body against Gunter. Her lips came close to his ear, and she whispered, "Today was a wonderful day. One of the best I have ever had. Thank you." She bit his earlobe and gave it a slight tug. As she released it, she said, "I love you."

Gunter wanted to say, "I love you, too," but strangely enough, it felt too easy. He didn't want to confess his feelings simply because she had. When he shared those intimate words, he didn't want to be elbow-deep in greasy water. He didn't want to merely respond in kind. He wanted the first time to be special. So, he did the only thing he could; he smiled, nodded his head a couple of times, and said, "I know," and then finished the roaster.

Bless her heart, Susan understood. She stepped back and waited for the roaster to be handed over for drying.

Ava's bark momentarily transported Gunter back to the wooded jungle. He reached down and petted her head and said, assuming she would understand, "If only we could pass under the branches, as you are able." As though comprehending Gunter's desire, Ava leaped past him and demonstrated how, with ease, she raced through the jungle and regained the lead from Dillon.

Gunter didn't need to labor to send his thoughts back to Minnesota. The Fourth of July, two and a half years after the Christmas party, Gunter sat with his arm around Susan, patiently waiting for the fireworks display. Anya, with a group of her girlfriends, played in the park, lacking the ability to sit and wait patiently. As Susan and Gunter made small talk, Gunter's hand periodically patted the outside of his pants pocket.

Tucked at the bottom of the pocket was a shiny, circular, gold object that just so happened to be the same radius as Susan's ring finger. Gunter was having two conversations simultaneously, one with Susan and another with himself, as he rehearsed the proposal.

With the first of a series of fireworks about to be launched into the dark sky, lit only by the twinkling of a handful of stars, Anya raced toward the blanket that kept Susan and Gunter off the damp grass. At the exact same moment, Gunter reached into his pocket and carefully slid the tip of his pinky finger into the ring. His hand was at the top edge of his jeans pocket when Anya, totally out of breath, reached them and mumbled a broken sentence. "Dad, Mom, can I ... watch the fireworks from the park ... with the other girls?"

The ring caught the lip of the pocket and aimlessly slipped from his finger and slowly worked its way to the bottom of the cotton sack, as

Gunter nodded that Anya's request was acceptable. He couldn't speak. He literally could not form any words. There was a void between his ears. In the time that it took to recover, he knew he couldn't marry Susan. The name Mom on the lips of Anya was more than he could bear. He also knew he would never tell Anya the truth of why things ended with Susan.

A month later, he finally had the courage to tell Susan that he didn't see them having a future. He enjoyed their time together. He found her interesting and certainly attractive, but truth be told, he was infatuated with her but not in love with her. It was not fair to lead her on with the hope that something more might become of their relationship.

A month later, to the day, Susan left the medical center. She left western Minnesota. She left the lives of Gunter and Anya, never to be heard from again.

Dillon, with his adolescent excitement, could hardly contain himself as he turned and faced the group and said, "I think I found the path that leads to the top. The rest of the hike should be considerably easier." It was obvious that Dillon was taking responsibility for the trek turning into a full day's journey.

Chuck was quick to offer a word of forgiveness in a non-direct manner. "Hey, not your fault that we are not familiar with Dusty's measurement of time and distance."

Unfortunately for Dillon and the labors of the others, the path was nothing more than a goat's path. Once out of the thickness of the trees, the climb was steep, and the footing was none too secure. They were climbing on small pieces of rock and shale that had broken off from higher elevations and were being pushed downward.

The only sounds for the next hour and forty-five minutes were Dillon's inquiry, "Everyone okay?" and the panting and huffing of the climbers, which grew in volume when rocks gave way beneath the hikers' boots and rattled and clanked down the mountain.

It was in the solitude, as a means of ignoring the pain that attacked her knee, as well as the dangers of the climb, that Anya attempted to answer her own question from the night before, "Whatever happened to Susan?" In the mind of an eight-year-old, she questioned if there was something she had done, or not done, something she said that caused Susan to leave them. She worked with the premise that Susan left them.

She can still vividly see the last day she saw Susan. It was a Saturday, and as had become the custom, Susan arrived in time for brunch. Anya's specialty was waffles, covered in whipped cream and coated with chocolate and strawberries. Depending on the weather, the three of them would play a game or hop in the car and take a drive. On that particular day, it was hot and muggy, and the beach was calling them. They drove to an area lake, where Anya spent the better part of the day swimming while Susan and Gunter napped and chatted as they lay on the sand.

Anya knew something was not right the moment they returned home. Susan wrapped her arms around her torso and hugged her. It was the sort of thing Susan did when she was preparing to leave, but it was time for dinner. She couldn't be leaving already. As Susan pulled back, Anya saw black streaks rolling down her cheeks. At first, she thought Susan must have hurt herself. She was crying. She was hurt. "Are you okay?"

"Yes, pumpkin, I'm fine. I just need to get going."

"But—but it soon will be time you eat. I am making—"

"I'm sorry, I can't stay tonight. I need to get going."

"But you always stay. I cook, and you and Dad eat and laugh and—"

Susan turned and walked toward the door, her shoulders shaking.

"Dad, Dad, come here. Susan is hurt. She is crying. She is leaving without her supper."

Still watching Susan clumsily push through the door and down the front steps, she didn't feel her dad's hand resting on her shoulder.

She jumped slightly when he spoke. "She loves you very much, Anya. Very much."

Oh, my god. Did that mean Susan didn't love Dad? Is that why he said those words in that manner? Anya started to lose her footing and slid to the edge of the cliff. Her legs were spread apart, and it felt as though she had one foot planted in the present and the other was rooted in the past, threatening to pull her over the edge. She was able to regain a position of stability and informed Brit, who was closest to her, that she was okay.

Breathing slowly and deeply, she focused herself and continued the climb. As she did, the words once again echoed in her thoughts. "She loves you very much, Anya." Anya never heard those words in that manner before. What rattled her was not that her dad spoke of Susan's love for her, but the thought that maybe Susan left them because she wasn't in love with her dad. How was it possible that someone didn't love her dad? That was the essence of her and her dad's relationship. She couldn't finish the thought for fear it might not be the truth.

She shook herself back into the present. She needed to focus on the here and now, as it was too dangerous not to pay attention. It was too dangerous not to carefully watch where one placed their feet. It was too dangerous to try to make sense of the present by focusing on the past. Yet Anya lifted her head to see that Dillon had stopped and was inviting the group to rest against a partially fallen tree.

"How are you doin', Dad?"

"Surprisingly well."

Anya wasn't surprised. Her dad took great pride in being physically fit and being able to keep up with athletes half his age. Unfortunately, he was unwilling to admit the wear and tear on his body. One would think a doctor should know better, but where the male ego is concerned, all logic is thrown out the window. "How about you? How are you doing?"

"Good until we started this last stretch. The added pressure of maintaining my balance on these rocks is making my knee sore."

Chuck quickly added, "I am so glad that Alice decided to stay behind. She never could have managed this. I'm not sure she would have made it through the woods."

Brit asked, "How are you doing, Chuck?"

"I'm winded, and my knees ache a bit as well, but I will go as long as I can."

Tilting his head back, using his hand to shield his eyes from the noontime sun, Dillon informed the group, "It's not too much farther now." With that, as only a mountain goat could do, he leaped across several loose rocks and was off. The group shuffled across those same rocks, resembling ninety-year-olds whose legs refused to stride forth.

Trusting her reaction time and that her feet would not willfully endanger her body, Anya allowed herself to consider the present by returning to the past. She had determined that such an approach to life was good not only for her but also for Gunter. He maybe just didn't realize it yet.

With her feet developing a rhythm of shuffling across the tops of the rocks, accompanied by the need to occasionally bend down to place her hand on the ground to keep from slipping, she dismissed the notion that Susan's departure was due to her not loving Gunter.

Likewise, she knew her dad well enough that she could read his body language, and it said, "I love you, Susan." Therefore, the only viable explanation for Susan's departure rested with her. She had to have done or said something that drove Susan away. And, away, not only from her but from her dad. No wonder he didn't want to talk about Susan. He didn't want to make her feel guilty. The pieces all fit in the giant puzzle. She was to blame for Susan leaving. She was to blame for her dad's life of loneliness. For a second time, she, and she alone, tore from her dad's life the woman he loved.

Having successfully crossed a three-foot-wide, extremely deep fracture on the face of the mountain that served as a water canal to carry the snow melt in the spring and heavy rains in the fall, the group awkwardly sat on an elk path and nursed from their water bottles. Sweat poured from their bodies as the afternoon sun baked the rocks. After five minutes of silence, Chuck spoke.

"I can't go much farther. I think I need to turn back."

Either Dillon misunderstood Chuck's request or elected to ignore it. "That's not a problem. Once we round the knob there," Dillon extended his arm, pointing off in the distance, "we will have made it to the top."

Everyone but Chuck turned and looked over their shoulder to see if the top was truly that close. None of them could see what appeared to be the top of the mountain. No one said a word.

Chuck earned his merit badge for hiking. He made it to the top, and he never complained that the summit was more than just around the bend. In fact, as they sat on a narrow strip of flat mountain top, eating the lunch Shatz had packed, it was Chuck who babbled endlessly.

As the group prepared to leave, Gunter noticed a geological marker pounded into a rock that stated the elevation as 8,250 feet.

Brit said, "I am pretty sure Round Creek Camp is 5,000 feet." No one said it, but each of them felt mighty proud of their accomplishment.

Before leaping down the mountain, Dillon announced, "I think I found the path we were supposed to take. We should be back in half the time it took us to get here." The others just smiled as though saying, "We'll wait and see."

The return trip was considerably shorter and, therefore, quicker but not necessarily less strenuous, and it certainly was not the path later described by both Shatz and Dusty. Sitting around the campfire later that evening, Dusty's comments about an easy hike and being only an hour and a half became the butt of many a joke. Something told everyone that those words would linger for the remainder of the trip.

Despite being on the verge of total exhaustion, once Gunter and Anya had zipped up their sleeping bags, both pulled out their book, switched on their headlamps, and read. The number of pages turned, however, was few. It was Gunter who first closed his book and turned off his light. Less than a page later, Anya followed suit. But before she permitted herself to drift off to sleep, she had to get something off her chest.

"Dad?" She whispered as she spoke. "You still awake?"

"Yeah. Everything okay?"

"I'm sorry for Susan leaving you." There was no way to lead into the things she wanted to share. It was best to just get to it.

"I don't understand. Sorry?" Even without seeing the wrinkling in his brow or his head that shook slightly, it was clear Gunter was confused.

"I drove her away and left you without the woman." Sobbing, her words left her momentarily.

Gunter didn't interrupt her. He waited patiently until she could finish. "Just like Mom, I—" She now wailed.

Having a sense of where this was headed, Gunter had to speak. "Anya, stop it. You did no such thing." He paused for a moment to make sure she could fully grasp what he was about to share. "Susan's leaving had nothing to do with you. As for your mother, that too wasn't your fault."

Not waiting to hear more, she spoke in between whimpers. "If it was not for me, she would be alive."

The volume of his voice increased in an attempt to be more persuasive. "You didn't cause your mom's death. It was a reaction to the drug. Her own body rebelled. Her own body deceived her in what should have been natural. The contractions never occurred."

"But, if it was not for me, there would not have been the need for the drug. Don't you see? I killed Mom!"

His throat swelled shut. Since that day thirty-eight years ago, he feared that Anya would feel she was responsible for Katharina's death. This was the first time she ever spoke the words aloud, but he was sure she felt them much earlier in life. His face was washed with his own tears. He wondered if her empathy, at such a young age, was her attempt to make right the wrong she concluded she had caused.

When he could breathe again, and words were able to be delivered, he spoke a truth he never uttered before. "Anya, even if that were true—which it's not—I would never give you up.

I can't conceive of life without you. The truth is, if anyone is responsible for Katharina's death, it's me."

"You? How?"

"How could I not see the signs? The moment your mom complained of a headache, I should have known."

"Don't be ridiculous"

"Ridiculous? Anya, your mom never got headaches, or if she did, she never spoke of them. A doctor, a good doctor, like a good scientist, pays attention, and even looks, specifically, for anything out of the ordinary. For anything that doesn't make sense. But I missed it because I was too caught up in the moment. Selfishly, I was more focused on myself and the excitement of becoming a dad than paying attention to your mom. Anya, if I had paid attention, if I had listened to your mom, she could be alive today."

The air inside the tent was thick and heavy, causing Gunter and Anya to struggle to breathe. The weight pressing upon them was guilt. Neither blamed the other for the tragedy that occurred in the hospital on the plains of Minnesota. They didn't need to, for each did that to themselves. The elephant in the room and in their daily lives, and in the past thirty-eight years, was now in the tent, and no simplistic word could or would undo that presence.

Just as Susan had departed all those years ago, leaving them alone with each other, so again, she was gone, and they were left with each other. Two individuals feeling guilty for the same event. An event neither caused nor had the ability to stop. There were circumstances beyond their control.

The elephant sat heavily upon them, threatening to expel all life from within each. Katharina, while physically gone, never really left either of them, and that was destroying their relationship. And, if truth be told, it was destroying them individually.

Chapter 5

Each rider looked longingly as they rode out of camp past the canvas-covered dining hall with its walls rolled up. They weren't sure what awaited them at the next campsite. Not even Jack, who had made many trips into the Bob Marshall Wilderness, had camped at Basin Creek.

As the guests busied themselves with packing up their belongings and taking down their tents, the wranglers were busy breaking down the camp, packing the mules, and saddling up the horses. The dew was heavy, making everything wet, but by the time the group was thirty minutes down the trail, the sun pulled the moisture from the top of leaves, horses, and boots.

Climbing out of the valley of Round Creek and meandering alongside Sun Creek, sometimes at water level and other times a hundred feet above, the scenery changed drastically. Literally, one's horse could have their front feet planted in one scene and back feet in another. An hour and a half into the morning, the riders found themselves in a part of the forest where wildfires had burned. Not once, but in some areas, twice. One, the result of lightning, and one, at the hand of humans.

It was eerie and picturesque, at the same time, to absorb acre after acre of nothing but blackened tree trunks scorched by the wildfires. The branches on the trees were gone, along with most of the ground cover, so that the fifty- and sixty-foot tree trunks looked like Lincoln Logs set on end. The wind moaned as it blew through large sections of wilderness, as though making a statement. One got the feeling that a lament was on the lips of the wind. Wind, herself, was equally responsible for the destruction and devastation of the forest. Once the flames came to life, they were pushed and carried by the wind. Yet, as revealed in Job's lament before God, it is always more complex than what first appears.

Wind alone cannot ignite a fire that grows into a flame. And if the wind attempts to harness its power and not blow, a fire has the capability to create its own wind. Wind is a tool in nature's rhythm of death and resurrection. Wind cannot make a seed germinate. Wind cannot nourish seedlings. But, without the wind, rain clouds would never move across the sky. Without the wind, the ground drenched in moisture would not dry. Wind is a tool in nature's rhythm of death and resurrection. She sings, she howls, and she has the power to destroy and the power to bring relief in a cool breeze. She is cursed when present and cursed when not. It probably is a good thing that wind is a tool of nature and not humanity.

This was the type of conversation one had during lunch with Dusty. The dialogue seemed to start with a simple question directed toward Dusty. His right hand washed over his face for a moment and ended at his chin just before he said, "Oh, I don't know." The truth was, he knew. He knew about a wide range of topics. Even the horses stood still when Dusty spoke. One could only wonder what wisdom they had gleaned from Dusty over the years. Or what wisdom he compiled from the horses.

Some forty minutes after mounting up, the troop of riders crossed the Continental Divide. A simple wooden sign to their right marked the location. It held two arrows carved into the plaque and the names of two flowing bodies of water. An arrow pointed to the right, the direction from which they just came, followed by the words, *Sun Creek*, and another pointed left, *Teton River*. It was so anti-climactic.

"That was it?" Alice spoke of what others were thinking.

Chuck followed the example of his wife in voicing his skepticism. "We're not even that high. How can this be the Continental Divide?"

Hearing the conversation unfolding behind him, Dusty softly applied pressure to the reins, and his horse stopped. He turned slightly in the saddle and waited for everyone to get close. He confirmed that the sign was correct. They just rode over the Continental Divide. He then added, "The Sun Creek flows to the east, and the Teton River flows westward. Contrary to the commonly held assumption, the Continental Divide is not necessarily the highest point. Rather, it is the hydrological divide that separates the flow patterns of the rivers on the continent. Most people assume there is one solid line that is connected from North America to South America, but actually, the Great Divide, which you just crossed, in Wyoming, in New Mexico, and in Mexico splits. The North American continent has six continental divides that determine if the water flows east or west, north or south. Personally, I think the Great Divide Basin in Wyoming is one of the most intriguing locations. Any precipitation that falls in that space does not flow east or west but remains in that basin. A basin that was created because the continental divide splits. The area, also known as the Red Desert, contains one of the largest herds of wild horses, elk, buffalo, on and on. It truly is unique."

Jack shared a bit of his own wisdom. "One of those six divides is located along the Appalachian Mountain Range. Bobby and I have ridden the Appalachian Trail many a time and crossed the Divide."

Bobby joined in the conversation, "That divide is a great example of a divide not having to be high in elevation. In northern Florida, where the Divide works its way south, the elevation is little more than seventy feet above sea level."

Twisting back in the saddle, Dusty picked up the reins, and his horse's ears tipped forward, and immediately he stepped off, pulling the mule along as they headed down the trail, westward, just as the Teton River flows.

Wasn't that representative of their relationship? Gunter's horse dropped in line behind Chuck, but he didn't really notice who he was following, for his thoughts were occupied. He wondered if the Continental Divide was the perfect metaphor for describing his relationship with Anya. They shared the same space, the same desires, the same dreams, and yet they seemed to flow in two different directions.

With the day's ride short in comparison to others, the group pulled into the Basin Camp a few minutes after two o'clock. The wranglers were busy setting up the makeshift canvas tent for the kitchen. The mules were already unloaded, and everyone's personal items were piled in a heap where they remained longer than one might expect. The horses were unsaddled and placed in the corral, where they, on cue, rolled out the stress of the ride while the riders drifted off together to find a shady spot to hydrate and stand around for a while to relieve the stress to their bottoms. As they consumed large amounts of water and described their favorite scenery from the ride, someone remembered Dusty, in passing, stating how the creek below the campsite was unusually warm, considering this campsite is typically the coldest in the morning. The conversation quickly shifted to those determining if they were brave enough to bathe in the creek and those who needed to locate their fly rods for a go at catching that "big elusive trout."

Bobby and Jack fished out their fly rods and tackle and met up with Dusty, who knew of a "secret" fishin' hole upstream. It was a place where the fish pulled from the water would push one's hands apart as they described the size of the one that got away. For some reason, the fish from that spot seemed to grow each time the tale was told. Quad and Dillon also determined that the warmth of the afternoon made for prime-time fishin'. But rather than join the old guys, they would skip their flies across the surface of the water at the bend in the creek upstream from the camp. It wasn't that they didn't appreciate the old guys; they just enjoyed the competition that existed between the two of them. They could turn any wrangler task into a competition, and neither of them liked to lose. Chuck, Alice, Gunter, and Anya decided the warm water could be put to better use and gathered up a towel and bathing items, while Brit and Shatz chose to find solitude behind their closed eyelids.

The word, *warm*, similar to the words, *an hour and a half*, was contextually dependent upon who said it. Since it was Dusty, everyone did not necessarily think that it was warm. Despite the chilly water temperature, Gunter found a bowl-like dip in the creek bottom, where he was able to lower his entire body into the water as though he was seated in a tub.

The eleven of them didn't come together until the call went out that the evening meal was ready. A warped table that leaned to one side provided space for eight plates and eight carefully balanced cups of people's beverage of choice. Dusty, Quad, and Dillon, the last to arrive, used their laps as tables and the ground to support their cups. Tales of the afternoon dominated the table talk.

Quad and Dillon were the first to excuse themselves as they left to prepare the herd to be released from the corral. Two horses were selected to remain behind to serve as mounts in the morning when Quad and another wrangler set out in search of the herd. A handful of the other horses and two mules were selected to wear bells that would alert the wranglers where they were located come morning. The process was known as jingling.

The moment the gate opened, the horses and the mules wasted little time in fleeing the campsite and making their way into the wilderness in search of grass. Dusty described, later that evening, while seated around the campfire, that it was not uncommon for the herd to cross the creek and make their way up the face of the mountain across from them.

Jack, who himself was full of stories about his own adventures in the wilderness, both in Montana and Georgia, prompted Dusty to share a time when the horses took off and were difficult to find, if at all.

With his weathered hand having covered his face and resting at his chin, Dusty began. "It wasn't too many years ago. Let me think, five years ago, three years before the fire that burned much of the territory we covered today, the herd crossed the ridge." His arm was raised, and his finger pointed to a spot across the valley, where with the light from the moon, one could see a slight dip in the tree line. "As I and another wrangler worked the mountainside, we heard a faint clanging. Sure enough, over the ridge and down into a pocket meadow, there was the herd, filling their bellies, except for two horses. We didn't locate those two horses and ended up completing the trip minus two horses. The spook didn't do us any good since it didn't keep the horses contained."

Chuck, in his customary spot, standing behind the group, who were seated around the campfire, interrupted Dusty. "Spook? What's a spook?"

"It's an item, usually a bag, we hang on the trail from which we came, to deter the horses from traveling back down the trail, should they make their way to the trail. In that situation, by crossing over the mountain, the horses bypassed the spook. A week later, at dusk, the two horses arrived back at the lodge. They walked up to the corral and waited to be noticed and placed in the corral."

"Have you ever had a horse die during a trip?" Chuck inquired.

"I haven't, but I know other outfitters have. Also, several years ago, during a trip, we encountered a group of riders that had a horse die on them."

Alice, who turned around and gave her husband a dirty look when he asked about horses dying, was pulled into the campfire story and, without forethought, asked, "What happened?"

"Never heard actually what happened."

Quad started to tell a story about the time a horse dropped during a trail ride, pinning the rider underneath the horse. He wasn't speaking very loudly, so it didn't seem rude when Jack spoke over him.

"What do you think, Bobby? Time to get the mouth organ out?"

Bobby's head dropped slightly so that the light of the fire couldn't catch his eyes beneath his black Stetson. But it didn't matter. Brit wasn't about to let Bobby hide. "Bobby, you play a harmonica?"

"I'm not sure I'd call it playin'." Bobby didn't raise his head as he answered. He didn't need to look up to know that ten pairs of eyes were looking directly at him. He could feel it, just as he was quite sure that nearly every face held a smile, with the biggest grin plastered on Jack's.

"Oh, come on, Bobby. You know that's not true. Hell, you've played on stage."

"Wait a minute. We have a musician in our midst, and we didn't know it?" Chuck moved closer to the circle as he spoke.

Bobby's hat tilted back, and he looked at the orange-shaded faces as he spoke. "Don't go gettin' carried away. I play a little guitar, and every now and then, for a song or two, I blow a few notes on a harmonica."

"Sounds to me like you're in a band." Gunter knew that Bobby's humility was legitimate. Just as he never once spoke of his horsemanship skills being something noteworthy, so he would downplay his musical abilities. Truth was, Bobby was a good horseman, and he didn't need to convince anyone he was.

"Yeah. I play with a few fellas."

"So, do you sing too?" Brit wasn't about to let it end until Bobby confessed.

"Well," the one-syllable word became three and dragged out until Bobby realized he wasn't going to get out of this. "We lost our vocalist, and I sing a few of the songs."

Gunter was sure "a few of the songs" meant all of the songs, but he didn't say anything.

"Where's this mouth organ we have heard about?" Chuck was careful not to say harmonica but used Jack's words as a way to become one of the guys.

With a toss of his head to the right, Bobby said, "It's in the tent."

"What are you waiting for? Go get it." Brit had no problem issuing the directive. With a heavy sigh, Bobby placed both hands on his knees and pushed himself up. The glow on his back diminished the farther he walked away from the campfire. Returning to the group, he carefully opened a small cardboard box and lifted a shiny silver harmonica. After tapping the instrument several times against the palm of his left hand, he wet his lips, brought the piece to his mouth, tilted it slightly to fit correctly, and began to play.

Five notes into the song, Gunter, Anya, and Shatz sang along. Before the end of the first verse, nearly everyone joined in to acknowledge that they, too, *once were lost but now were found.*" Singing "Amazing Grace" offered more warmth to the bodies around the fire than the fire itself. Once the sun was buried behind the mountain, Basin Creek lived up to the label of being the coldest campsite.

The next offering was "Home on the Range." Before a third song could be played, voices from the group made requests. Some were played, and some were not. Those not played were because Bobby didn't know them.

As the logs gave away and the fire started to die down, Bobby said, "One more."

Gunter, who had not made a single request, was the first to speak. "I Will Always Love You."

"Yeah, that's a good one to end with. But just so you all know. I do the original, Dolly's version."

Gunter quickly added, as though totally surprised, "There's another?"

Everyone laughed, and the sweet sound filled the night air. No one said anything as the final note was carried to the highest peak.

One by one people drifted from the circle, leaving Gunter to stare alone at the flames that danced back and forth between a blue and red tint. It was only a matter of minutes before the ashes consumed the flame, and thick, suffocating smoke bellowed upward until it reached the treetops, where the northwest breeze pushed the smoke across the valley. It occurred to Gunter for the first time that the source, the fuel for the fire, eventually became the fire's demise. With the tip of his worn-out boots, he poked at the ashes and blew a puff of air to ignite the fire. A flame leaped forth only to grow dim and fade completely. It troubled him that life might be just like a fire. The fuel, the source of one's existence, might be the cause of one's death. Was it possible that the very thing that gave meaning to life could also consume life? Suffocate one? In the darkness of the night, Gunter feared that life might be nothing but an endless series of darkness.

By the time Gunter crawled through the opening of the tent, Anya's headlamp was no longer lit. Her breathing was deep and rose and fell in a consistent rhythm. She didn't need to ask the question that was on the lips of her fellow travelers: "Why the song, 'I Will Always Love You'?" She knew the answer. She had heard the story many times before. It was one of those stories that defined their family.

Burying himself in his sleeping bag, Gunter never opened the pages of *Out of the Wild*, for he had his own story to carry him into the night. The images tucked behind his eyelids were as vivid as if the events happened yesterday.

The story started at the same moment every time it was replayed, a week before first-semester finals or two weeks before Christmas. Gunter was sporting a crush on one of the girls who was part of a group that hung out together on weekends.

Gunter couldn't keep from staring in her direction whenever the group assembled. He wasn't the only male who found the blonde-haired girl with soft brown eyes and two dimples that made an appearance whenever she smiled—which was just about always—easy on the eyes. Her voice was pleasing to the ear, and when she spoke, everyone seemed to listen. The only difference between Gunter and the other males in the group was that Gunter had never actually had a one-on-one conversation with the young lady he thought was a model.

It took thirteen weeks for Gunter to finally get enough nerve to speak directly to the woman whose figure was made for a two-piece swimsuit. The problem for Gunter was that the purpose for speaking with this "angel" with a slightly upturned nose that accentuated her femininity, was to ask her out. It was a problem because, as far as he knew, no other male had been successful in convincing Katharina to go out with them. The idea of a date with the most beautiful woman on campus, if not on the face of the earth, was overwhelming.

He had started practicing the speech he would use the second time he saw her. Their first encounter was too much for him to consider anything but her grace and poise. He practiced in front of the mirror to ensure that he didn't look too dorky, but he looked dorky, nervous, like a minor leaguer trying to pass himself off as someone ready for the big leagues.

The pictures in his mind, forty-five years later, were so real, so powerful that his hands, tucked inside the sleeping bag, were clammy, and tiny beads of sweat rolled from his armpits. Gunter found himself alone with Katharina on Sunday evening in the foyer of the dormitory, the designated location for those wishing to walk over to the cafeteria for the evening meal. After three deep breaths, he stumbled forth. "Katharina, I—I was wondering if you wanted to go to the movie—the movie on Friday. Not a date or anything, but well, you know, kinda a date."

Two dimples appeared as she reached out and touched the sleeve of his coat. "I would like that."

Gunter had no idea how he survived the week. Friday evening couldn't come fast enough. The movie, for their viewing, was sponsored by the college and was projected on a huge screen in the gymnasium. Students brought blankets and pillows and laid on the wooden floor. Concluding he was out of her league, he didn't even attempt to hold her hand during the movie. The film starred Dustin Hoffman, who played Lenny Bruce, a controversial comedian who died in 1966 due to an accidental overdose of acute morphine poisoning. It wasn't what one might call a date movie, but it did provide plenty of topics to discuss afterward.

Following the movie, the couple hit a dive bar, where the drinks were cheap, and no one paid attention to who rang the bell above the door when they entered. Selecting the corner booth and protected by the high back, they discussed the movie, the end of the semester, and their plans for the Christmas break. Gunter soon forgot he was nervous, and together they spoke as longtime friends.

As his second glass of beer was nearly gone, Gunter heard himself asking the young woman across from him if she liked to dance.

"I love to dance." There wasn't a moment's hesitation before the words swept across the sticky tabletop.

Gunter slid across the vinyl seat and stepped away from the booth and his date, only to stop abruptly and look back over his shoulder. "Any particular song you want to dance to? I'll see if it's in the jukebox."

With one swift move, she stood next to him with her arm casually wrapped around his. She said, "No, you pick. I will dance to anything."

Feeding a quarter into the silver machine, Gunter pushed B-5. Cupping Katharina's right hand and softly placing his right arm around her waist, the two of them stood on the tiny dance floor tucked next to the bar, waiting for the forty-five to drop and play. Red and blue lights alternated, blinking from the jukebox as Dolly Parton's voice whispered the first verse only to grow into the refrain, *"But I will always love you."*

Before the night ended and Gunter walked Katharina to the door of her room on the fourth floor, he had spent a dollar fifty on B-5. Deep in his sleeping bag, remembering their first kiss, he whispered to no one but himself, "I'd spend a million fifty to have one more dance with my angel."

Chapter 6

It has been thirty-eight years since he last held Katharina, yet many nights while he slept, he could feel her body tight against his, and he could inhale the scent that was uniquely her. As a tactile person, touch was not only important, but it was also a necessity. She needed to touch and be touched. It was a trait passed on to Anya.

When Gunter and Katharina were first married, he could never figure out why the candles in the house were dented with tiny marks. It wasn't until he saw Katharina pressing her nails into the wax that he realized the source of the dents. That knowledge served him well when Anya was two and a half years old, and he noticed the candles in the house bore a similar imprint.

The first time they made love, Katharina demanded that they not get dressed but stay next to each other, naked. Gunter had remained at her side for what he considered to be a long time. He rolled away from her and sat on the edge of the bed, pulling on his pants, when her arm reached around his chest and pulled him back to her body. She whispered, with the same breathy tone that Dolly used as she sang, and asked, "Where are you going? I want you to stay with me." As the years passed, Gunter wanted to remain next to her, for he, too, grew to love the touch. He hated to wake up and realize it had all been a dream.

Her smell, her voice, and her touch all felt so real. That morning was no different.

So many times, when she came to visit him in his dreams, they talked. She listened and he spoke. Like the way he spoke to her the night of Anya's birth. Other times, he listened as she spoke. Many visits, most visits, focused on Anya. Gunter knew that Anya needed a woman's perspective, but not just any woman. She needed a mom. Unfortunately, in Gunter's mind, there was only one mom—Katharina. During those challenging adolescent years, Katharina and Gunter spoke nearly every night. It was on her eighteenth birthday that Gunter confessed in his dream that he didn't want to disappoint Anya in the same way he disappointed Katharina when she needed him most. Therefore, he pulled back. He had been pulling back for the last eighteen years. He knew it was wrong, but …

Rubbing the grit from the corners of his eyes, he peered at his watch. The illuminated hands revealed that it was 5:33. He needed to pee. Pulling on his boots, he stepped from the tent. The brisk temperatures needled his face, and he hoped it would be enough to distract him from the dream that followed him. With the zipper to his pants properly positioned, he left the clump of trees he used to shield his body and slowly walked toward the tent. His breath warmed his face, and he realized that the temperature could not freeze his thoughts.

Standing some twenty yards from the tent that held the most precious thing in his life, he looked upward, past the stars that were quickly losing their power, as the sun was climbing the ridge of the mountain and into the heavens. He just stood there, staring, unable to reach out and touch or be touched, for he stood alone. Alone! So, terribly alone! But what pained him more was hearing in his dream Katharina's voice that said, "Oh my dear. It has not been eighteen years. You have been pulling back for the past thirty-eight years. You must stop this now, or you will lose her forever. FOREVER."

The sound of the zipper opening on Bobby and Jack's tent, some thirty yards beyond Gunter's tent, ripped Gunter from his statue-like state. He cursed silently just as he did when his bladder awoke him, for Katharina never told him how he could stop pulling back. "Dammit," was the only word he had to offer. "Dammit."

Before he left the tent to go in search of coffee, he made sure Anya was awake. It was another travel day, and the crew would need their personal items and tent shortly after breakfast.

"How'd you sleep?"

"Not well. You kept tossing and turning, and that woke me up. Were you dreaming?" "Dreaming?" Gunter shrugged his shoulders. "I suppose I was if I was that restless.

But I don't remember anything."

"I wish I had that problem. I remember my dreams too clearly." Gunter smiled.

"Boy, does that bring back memories."

"Oh, yeah? How so?"

"Daddy, Daddy, come here." Gunter used falsetto to mimic a young child. "I had a bad dream."

"What, you never had a nightmare?"

"I didn't say that. I was merely recalling how, for an extended period, your dreams were vivid and caused you to awaken. For a moment in time, you couldn't discern dream from reality."

Gunter, atop his sleeping bag, and Anya, buried up to her neck in hers, were silent. Without planning it and without realizing it, the two of them were about to address a critical piece of their relationship. The key factor would be whether they could be honest with each other and themselves.

"Do you ever dream about Mom?"

The inside of the tent went dark, darker than any night void of the moon, darker than a windowless basement, darker than the inside of a sealed casket. Gunter questioned if they might still be asleep, and this was a dream. Was it possible that he never left the tent to pee, never stood staring into the heavens, never heard Bobby and Jack's tent zipper from the outside of the tent, and had yet to wake Anya? It was all a part of his current dream, and therefore, he was dreaming that Anya inquired about Katharina. But why? Why would he do that to himself? Why persecute himself with such a question? Of course, he dreamed about Katharina nearly every night, but that's not something a father shares with his daughter, who never met her mom. To admit to such a thing would only compound her sadness. Surely, she can't dream about her mom.

He felt a chill from the breeze that blew past the open flap. He didn't close it upon his return. This wasn't a dream. The best answer was to say "yes" and then suggest they pack up their belongings before breakfast. But he knew his daughter, and she would never settle for just the word *yes*. She would want details. And honestly, he wasn't ready to go down that trail. How could he explain that he was dependent upon Katharina's visits? Together they discussed how best to raise their daughter. Her own mom, less than an hour earlier, told him that if he continued to pull back, he would lose his daughter, and here he was, pulling back. But what choice did he have?

The wind increased, and as it pushed through the trees, it sang a simple verse. "*I wish you joy ... happiness. I wish you love.*" The words filled the tent, and Gunter couldn't avoid the truth. There would be no joy, no happiness without love. And in love, he must speak the truth.

Nodding his head several times, he looked directly at his daughter and said, "Yeah." A smile accompanied the rest of his answer. "Many times have I dreamed about your mom."

Without a moment's hesitation, Anya said, "So have I."

Every bit of air escaped from his lungs. It was like the time a horse bucked him off, and he greeted the ground with such force that he had the wind knocked out of him. Tears formed in his eyes, not because he couldn't breathe but because he was overwhelmed. He never imagined that Anya would dream about her mom. The shock of her words was too much. He couldn't. He just couldn't. All he could get out was, "I need to get some coffee."

The pancakes didn't want to go down, coffee invoked a gag reflex, and swallowing was next to impossible because of the feelings and thoughts welling up from within. Gunter was the first to dismiss himself from breakfast and begin the task of dismantling the tent. He volunteered to assist with saddling the horses and then made his way to the kitchen to help Shatz tear down the cooking stove and pack up the kitchen. He needed to keep himself occupied until he could settle in the saddle and use the rhythm of his horse to grapple with the words, "So have I."

The train of riders mounted their four-legged companions and prepared to leave camp with the wranglers left behind to finish the final wrapping of the panniers that carried the kitchen supplies. Gunter informed Anya that he was going to take the tail of the string in order to work on a few things with his horse, but the truth was that he needed to work on himself. He was mildly surprised when Anya never questioned his decision, but simply said, "Okay." Bringing up the rear provided a very different perspective to the train of riders.

Gunter found himself staring at the feet of those ahead of him, which surprised even him. He had never considered what one might conclude about a rider's skill, level of comfort, and overall horsemanship by paying attention to the foot in the stirrup. His initial observation was that no two riders carried their feet in the stirrup exactly the same manner or position. This realization made him think about his own foot placement, and eventually, his head tilted left and then right to observe his own feet. Before the distance became too great between him and the rest of the riders, he attempted to draw some conclusions.

Contrary to the suggestion that Bobby's horse would need the encouragement of spurs, the heel of Bobby's boots, carrying spurs, never turned inward toward his horse's sides. Alice's foot was deep in the spur, making her heel higher than the toe of hiking boots. Chuck's heels were slightly pressed downward, but his feet appeared heavy as though pressing down upon the stirrups. It was no surprise that Alice's knees ached, and Chuck's bottom was numb from time to time. The ball of Anya's foot was properly placed on the stirrup, and her heel was slightly lower than her toe. However, trying to stay soft and light in the saddle was causing her feet, from time to time, to move from side to side in the stirrups. No doubt, that movement was aggravating an old weight-lifting injury on the inside of her knee.

Jack probably should have requested to use Bobby's spurs, as his heels were consistently finding his horse's side, and still, the horse didn't move out of low gear.

Acknowledging to himself that the monitoring of his fellow companions' foot placement was simply an avoidance technique, Gunter leaned back slightly in the saddle and prepared himself to contemplate the meaning and consequences of Anya's words, "So have I." However, the trip along the banks of the Teton River offered yet another distraction. Much of the area halfway between Basin Camp and the ranger's station had been burned by the 2017 fire. As a result, when the snow melted and the spring rains fell, the raging waters climbed the banks and cascaded against the dead trees. Like tinker toys pummeled by a dog's tail, the trees mercilessly collapsed. In some places, the height of a fallen tree made the trail impassable. At other locations, the debris covering the trail resembled a giant spider's web. The trail was passable but less than safe for both horse and rider, and it was certainly not safe for the pack animals that were still to come.

Dusty, with a trail saw in hand, went to work on the tree covering the trail, cutting a section wide enough to accommodate the pack mules. The rest of the crew tackled the spider web of branches and smaller tree trunks. By the time the spider web no longer offered a threat, Dusty had sawed through one side of the tree. Chuck jumped into action and volunteered to put his muscles to work sawing the other side. Bobby and Gunter struggled to lift the massive trunk upward so the saw wasn't pinched. With their bodies drenched in sweat, the teeth of the saw ripped through the bark on the underside of the tree, and a four-foot section of the tree dropped to the ground. With the log rolled to the side of the trail, the riders were able to continue their trek toward the ranger's station until they encountered another area littered with fallen trees.

The sight of the ranger's station in the distance invoked an audible sigh of relief from three of the seven riders. The location had been preselected as the site for lunch and a thirty-minute break. However, with aching knees and bottoms, now accompanied by shoulders, biceps, and triceps, the hope was that thirty minutes would be stretched to forty-five, with enough time to eat and adequate time to take a quick catnap. By this juncture in the trip, each guest felt comfortable sharing an idea or making a request of Dusty, knowing that as long as it didn't endanger horses or humans, he would more than likely grant the request. If he didn't, he would have a valid explanation.

The ranger's station, in the middle of the wilderness, complete with a corral, was quite a facility. Crude and rugged, yet accommodating and hospitable. The outhouse was the masterpiece of the entire camp. Positioned behind the ranger's shack and some forty feet above, it provided a spectacular view. With the door left open, an individual seated on the "throne" could look across the river below to the face of the mountain on the other side. It gave new meaning to sitting on the throne and viewing one's kingdom.

The horses were tied to the hitching post and the cinches loosened. The sound of crinkling sandwich baggies filled the porch of the ranger's shack. All seven riders found a spot on the porch to rest as they quietly consumed the lunch Shatz packed for each of them. It was the hump day of the excursion, and it showed in the body language. Breathtaking scenes that just the day before would result in fingers pointing or heads turning to absorb the entirety of nature before one's horse carried them to the next bend or tree that blocked the view were viewed with minimal gestures. Rather than consciously positioning their bodies so as not to exclude anyone, should a conversation break out, everyone merely dropped to a position that offered comfort. No one was intentionally being rude; it was simply hump day. The group had developed an identity that was rooted in respect that each individual was a member of the group and trust that each individual would be protected by the group.

With a skeleton key in hand, Dusty asked if anyone was interested in stepping inside the shack. No one needed a second invite. Standing in a lopsided circle in the center of the one-room shack, each person commented on a different item from the dark space. The shelves were stocked with canned goods, while the walls held the necessary tools to make survival in the wilderness possible. A narrow loft above the entrance held bunk beds. Relics and antiques were the norm, but their value was not in being sold or traded but in their usefulness. The station wasn't meant to provide permanent housing but a wayward location, a sanctuary from the elements, a place to gather for respite. Therefore, the sliver of light that pierced through the roof was not deemed critical. No one spoke as they slowly exited the shack, yet the consternation painted on each face suggested that a new appreciation for rangers was instilled. The romanticism of the profession got a little bit tarnished and dirty.

Dusty stood on the porch and spoke to no one and everyone, "The mules should be passing through in another fifteen or twenty minutes. We'll stick around for another fifteen minutes after they leave." In response to Dusty's update, they all went their separate ways. Some attempted to sleep, others took a hike, and others found a comfortable backrest and enjoyed the warmth of the sun.

Seventeen minutes later, the train of mules and four wranglers lumbered into the ranger's station. Under the guidance of Quad, the group stopped momentarily to speak with Dusty. Only Shatz dismounted and scampered up the hill behind the ranger's shack. The mules stood patiently waiting for the pressure to their halter to inform them that it was time to move forward. The exception was a black mule. His hind legs were in constant movement. A dance of sorts was being performed. It was harmless until the moment he kicked out at the mule tethered to him. Quad, with a flex of his wrist, tightened the tethered rope that was connected to the black mule's halter, which brought the mule's nose up slightly and forced the mule forward in search of the release. The moment the mule stepped forward, Quad relaxed his wrist, eliminating the pressure on the mule's face, and the mule stood still.

When Shatz returned, Quad tossed the lead rope toward her and said, "You take this string the rest of the way. I'll take your four."

"Does that mean I get to lead?"

With some reluctance, Quad agreed to let Shatz take the point and guide them into camp, even though he knew Dillon would never let him hear the end of that decision. With the lead rope secured to the horn of her saddle, Shatz took the point. Quad directed his horse in behind Shatz's string of mules, and Dillon, already mocking Quad, made sure he was ahead of Brit.

"What's the matter, Quad? You need a girl to show you how to lead that string? Are those mules too much for you to handle? Need a cowgirl to take over?" A quarter mile out from the ranger's station, Dillon was still jawing away. His laughter, which was contagious, filled the valley like a morning fog. Those left behind at the station, not asleep, found themselves laughing as well.

No one said it, but one couldn't help wondering if Quad's action was a part of the cowboy flirtation. There certainly had to be a code for how a cowboy flirted. One couldn't just come right out and say, "I think you're cute." One couldn't be too obvious or allow themselves to be too vulnerable. Plus, what could speak louder about what one was feeling than to hand over a pack of mules and give up the point? If that doesn't say, "Hey, I like you and would like to spend some time gettin' to know you," nothing else would.

Some fifteen minutes after the wranglers headed down the trail, everyone was in the saddle, and Dusty weaved his horse and mule between the group and nodded that it was time to go. As Dusty rounded the corral to return to the trail, something caught the attention of his horse and pulled the horse's head in the direction of the river below them. Like choir members following the direction of the conductor, the other six horses, in unison, also turned and looked toward the river. It took another minute for the eyes to see what the ears heard. From the river, a hiker emerged. With a slight tug of the reins, seven horses stopped, and seven adults stared at the figure.

The hiker was the first to speak. "Hey, there! Can you tell me the name of this spot?

And, how far to Canada?"

Dusty fielded the gentleman's questions while the others continued to stare. Two locations on the man pulled the eyes of the six like a magnet. One was his face, more specifically, his beard. The gentleman's beard was both long and wide. The length nearly exceeded his sternum, and the width was twice the size of his head. The other location was roughly six inches above his kneecaps. The plaid kilt was not the standard Western dress, but it was a common uniform among hikers walking the Continental Divide from Mexico to Canada. The smiles revealed the question, "Do you think there are any undergarments beneath that kilt?" The answer more than likely was, nope!

The conversation revealed that he left Mexico on the eleventh of May, and now, on the twenty-first of August, he was within three days of Canada. He was proud that he wasn't among those who were behind him. He wasn't the first to finish the hike, but he also wasn't among those who, well, were slow.

Everyone, each in turn, wished him well as they lifted the reins and nudged their horse forward. There was an unspoken relief that the hiker hadn't emerged from the river twenty minutes earlier. It might have been embarrassing to compare the string backpack he carried and the string of mules that carried supplies for the group on horseback.

Leaving the ranger's station behind, the density of the forest established the temperament of the afternoon ride. Even though the sun was shining, no shadows were being cast. It was impossible to see much farther into the wilderness, either to the right or left, than fifteen to twenty feet. There were occasions when a patch cleared in the treetops, and if one looked, just at the right moment, a mountain peak in the distance appeared. Matching the landscape, a somberness engulfed the group. No one spoke, no one gestured toward a breathtaking sight. Even the horses became melancholy with their heads dropped low, and yet not one tried to grab a mouthful of grass. It became a reflective, thoughtful, meditative ride.

Gunter took advantage of the solitude to return to Anya's words, which stirred both within his belly and brain: "So have I." *I wonder*, his thoughts began, *how does one dream about that which one has never seen? What does she see? Do they converse, or is it merely an image that appears? Are the dreams positive or nightmares?* Gunter's horse stopped in the middle of the stream to get a drink, and the absence of movement startled him. He wasn't aware that they had entered the water. His thoughts had shifted from his daughter's dreams to his own. His horse stood alongside Jack's horse, and for all Gunter knew, Jack might have attempted to converse with him, but his ears could only hear the words inside his head.

Katharina never aged. Her thick, wavy brown hair never thinned, and it never turned gray. Her smooth skin remained wrinkle-free, while with each visit, Gunter's face gave birth to another crease, another fold, a deeper furrow. She always arrived wearing the navy floral dress that he had purchased for the funeral. Her figure returned to that of their wedding night, each curve perfectly in proportion to the next. As for his, gravity was winning the battle.

As his horse climbed the bank, exiting the stream, he instinctively leaned forward.

Gunter recognized that he had never considered that the woman who came to visit him was the woman he knew forty years earlier. Why would he question it? It was the woman he loved and cherished, the woman he assumed he would grow old next to, the woman who would laugh and cry with him, the woman who would challenge him and support him, the woman who would give birth. He stopped himself. Katharina remained a twenty-seven-year-old, yet the wisdom she shared was that of a wise old sage. It gave him pause to wonder, just what was the source of his dreams?

Dreams?

Gunter was well aware that the number of books written covering the topic of dreams could easily fill several bookshelves in any local library. It wasn't unusual for patients to schedule a doctor's appointment due to a dream. Similarly, while making early morning rounds at the hospital, he would encounter a patient who shared a dream from the previous night and inquired, "What does it mean?" Yet, the most insightful work on dreams, at least for Gunter, came from two episodes from the TV sitcom *M*A*S*H*. The first episode was entitled "Hawk's Nightmare," and the second was "Dreams."

The first episode begins with Hawkeye, named after the main character in his father's favorite book, *The Last of the Mohicans*, standing over an operating table, commenting on the soldier he is feverishly laboring to save. "They're babies." After more than twelve hours of surgery, Hawkeye drops onto his cot, exhausted. Before long, he is up and walking about the camp, playing a game of basketball, minus the ball, and shooting marbles, minus the marbles. When he encounters fellow soldiers, Hawkeye refers to them as though they are his childhood friends. Hawkeye is sleepwalking; he dreams of being back in his hometown as a young lad playing with his best friends. Ushered back to his cot, still dreaming of Crabapple Cove, the carefree frolicking with buddies turns dangerous, and Hawkeye awakens from the nightmare convinced his friends are in danger. Night after night, similar scenes play out with Hawkeye dreaming of innocent encounters with childhood buddies, which, at some point, go horribly wrong and result in him awakened by his screaming.

Sidney, a psychiatrist, is summoned to meet with Hawkeye. Sidney's evaluation of his friend, Hawkeye, concludes with the following conversation: Sidney said, "You're making it all the way back to Crabapple Cove. All the way back to a time when playing ball and shooting marbles and going to picnics were all there was to worry about. No more responsibility."

"No more life and death decisions."

Sidney adds to Hawkeye's observations, "And the pain was a skinned knee."

"What about my nightmares?"

"What about them?"

"I keep having these dreams about these kids I grew up with, and I—" Hawkeye stops himself for a moment. "The dreams start out okay. The kids are fine. And then they end in disaster. Like those kids who roll past you on that bloody assembly line. You dream to escape, but the war invades your dream, and you wake up screaming. The dream is peaceful. Reality is the nightmare."

Gunter, having committed every episode of *M*A*S*H* to memory, replayed two key sentences as he continued to ride through the wilderness. "You dream to escape" and "Reality is the nightmare." Did he dream to escape the reality of life? Were his nightly encounters with Katharina simply an escape? Did Anya use her dreams in the same manner?

The first year following Katharina's death was a nightmare. Conversing with her in his dreams was a means of keeping her present. It was a way to survive, to cope with a reality that didn't make sense. It was a way to escape. As the years grew in number, from that pivotal day late in May, Gunter no longer viewed reality as a nightmare, yet Katharina continued to appear.

Gunter's horse slipped to the right as the rocks beneath his hooves grumbled. For a moment, reality stood still as Gunter wasn't sure if his horse would be able to regain his footing and avoid sliding down the hundred-foot-plus drop. Gunter pressed his knees inward against the saddle to maintain his balance. If the horse was going to drop, he decided he would drop with the animal. Fortunately for both, the horse was able to find solid footing with several quick, short steps to the left. And then, as though nothing happened, the horse continued forward.

The sudden and unexpected movement of his horse caused him to question if he had been honest throughout the years concerning his definition of reality. Did reality stand still beyond the boundaries of the first year? Had reality become something other than a nightmare? Was the analogy of slipping on loose rocks descriptive of his life covering the last thirty-eight years? Was that also how Anya was feeling?

Breathing deeply, with his heart rate returning to normal, Gunter wondered if perhaps the second episode from *M*A*S*H* might shed light on his perceived reality and dreaming. The medical staff was working a third straight shift. They were overtaxed, exhausted, and, at a certain level, experiencing fatigue. Unable to take an extended break due to the wounded continuing to arrive, staff members took catnaps, just long enough to enter into a state of dreaming. Similar to the first episode, each dream starts out positive but, at some point, turns into a nightmare. Hawkeye, the protagonist, is left without arms as he falls asleep during training to learn how to reattach limbs. He was set afloat on a small boat in the middle of a river. Washed ashore, he walks up to a gurney bearing a Korean child desperately in need of medical attention. Hawkeye, without any arms, is unable to perform the necessary procedures to save the young child. The only thing he can do is scream at the top of his lungs, which awakens him to the truth that more wounded are awaiting his services.

Gunter memorized every episode of the series because *M*A*S*H* was the inspiration behind his desire to become a medical professional. Even though Hawkeye was a fictional character, Gunter was not that far removed from the character. He found himself at Katharina's bedside, without any arms, because selfishly, he put his needs ahead of his wife's. All Gunter could do was scream.

He lifted the reins, and his horse stopped. He sat there at the tail end of the string of riders and slowly turned his head, first to the right and then left. Wave after wave of landscape cascaded down upon him, but he didn't see it. His vision narrowed. It was like peering through a scope attached to a rifle, and off in the distance was a tiny speck. A speck that grew as it moved closer and closer until it filled the entirety of the lens. The speck was transformed into Katharina. Her body was covered with a white sheet. The only part visible was her head. The body continued to move closer and closer. The size of her head was distorted. Her hair disappeared, and then her ears, followed by her eyes and nose. The only thing visible were her lips. The last place he touched her before the sheet entombed her body. But this time his lips were not pressed together in preparation to touch her. Instead, there was a chasm from which his lungs expelled air. He screamed!

In reality, the scream never escaped his thoughts. The sound he actually heard originated from someone up ahead, who yelled, "Elk! Elk in the water!"

Several hundred feet below them was a buck elk. A zoom lens from a camera revealed that the massive animal was face down in the water. One side of his large horn rose above the water, with the other side submerged. A lone voice asked, "How did that happen?"

No one spoke initially. The truth was, there was no answer, merely an educated guess. Dusty, Bobby, and Jack offered up guesses. Any of them or none of them may have been the truth.

As Gunter listened, he came to understand that was reality. Sometimes in dreams and in daily life, there are no answers, merely educated guesses. It was the reality he had been living for the past thirty-eight years without discernment. As the group rode on, still considering the elk's demise, Gunter pondered the question: "Is it possible to create a new reality?"

Chapter 7

Selecting the perfect location for the placement of the tent encompasses more than finding a flat site. There are several factors to be considered prior to spreading out the tent and driving stakes into the ground. A spot may appear flat, but without getting down on one's hands and knees, a rock, the presence of which will result in discomfort during the middle of the night, may be missed. The ground may pass the hands and knees test, but what about the setting? Are there tree branches overhead? If so, do the branches appear sturdy enough to withstand a storm? Will the tent be situated downwind or upwind from the horses and mules? What is the proximity of other tents? How far is the kitchen? And perhaps most important of all, where might the green tepee be positioned?

Ah, the green tepee. A luxury in the middle of the wilderness. It was the last structure to be erected at the campsite, even though many of the riders needed its presence the moment their foot touched the ground. The placement and construction of the green tepee fell to Quad and Dillon. With their other duties completed, they took up a green tarp, a box, three long branches, and a shovel, and the two wranglers marched out of camp a short distance. The moment the two returned to camp, a steady stream of people visited the green tepee. To everyone's surprise, upon their very first visit to the green tepee, atop the wooden box, the height of which was eighteen inches, rested a padded toilet seat. That first afternoon and evening, most guests thought the padded seat was a bit much, but come Monday morning, when the thermometer read thirty-five degrees, people's bottoms were thankful for the padding.

Anya had mentally prepared herself to carry a shovel into the woods. Gunter had warned her that there would be no mini biffs in the wilderness. She acknowledged, more than once during the fifteen-hour road trip, that this was one aspect of the trip she never considered. Therefore, shortly after they arrived at Round Creek on Sunday afternoon and witnessed the construction of the green tepee, Anya was relieved that this was one less thing she needed to negotiate. Knowing that they would be spending two nights at the campsite, Gunter and Anya carefully selected the location for their tent. They were satisfied with their selection once the green tepee was erected.

"There is only one way to properly break in a new pair of boots."

"What's that?" Anya, wearing a newly purchased pair of hiking boots, was curious to discover the proper technique. Considering the added stress to her credit card, she wanted to ensure that her boots lasted a good long time.

Chuck was moderately surprised that someone picked up on his open-ended comment and sought clarity. That hadn't always been the case. It wasn't that others were intentionally being rude; it was more to the fact that some of Chuck's comments seemed so out of context, making it difficult to know what to say.

The conversation had started with Dusty reminding the group that tomorrow was a fishing day for anyone interested. Bobby, under the glow of the campfire, mourned the demise of his ill-fated fishing boots during their last outing, which brought laughter to the circle. Everyone could still see the sole of his boot, attached only at the heel, flapping like the wings of a duck as he removed the boot. Followed by Dillon's quick-witted comment, "No wonder you didn't bring any fish back; you scared them all away."

Bobby then concluded, "I guess I will have to wear my riding boots and hope the glue holds."

It was at that point that Chuck offered his comment as he stood behind Anya and Brit. Anya turned to look at him and asked, "What's that?"

Smiling, Chuck was enthusiastic with the reply. "You wear them into the shower."

For several seconds, there was total silence, and eyes darted about the campfire. The image was overwhelming, in part, because Chuck was standing just as he would be standing in the shower, minus his clothes, of course.

It was Anya who, again, turned and spoke directly to the man standing behind her. "You're joking, right?"

"No, that's how you break in a new pair of army boots."

Everyone erupted into laughter except for Alice, who glared at Chuck.

Despite the laughter, Chuck continued to describe, in detail, how the water softened the leather of the boot, and that set the stage for a light-hearted mood around the campfire until Jack, during a period when everyone's eyes were drawn to the flames, turned to Gunter and asked a serious question.

"Hey, Doc." It was the first time anyone on the trip called Gunter, Doc. His buddy back home did, and it felt right to Gunter because he knew it originated out of respect for the vocation. Jack's use of the title, Gunter concluded, was also rooted in respect for the duties that doctors perform. Gunter listened intently as Jack finished. "I have always wondered what's it like for a doctor to lose patients. I assume you have had a few die."

Anya pulled back from the heat of the fire without realizing she moved. Jack's question, by itself, created more than enough heat. She had never heard this question put to her dad. It wasn't the notion or image of patients dying that concerned her. If Anya knew a patient of Gunter's who had passed away, he told her. What concerned her was the connection to her mom. She feared that he might go directly to Katharina's death. She didn't want anyone to pity her. Besides, her mom's death was just as much her story as his, and if she wanted that made public, it was up to her to tell it. She held her breath as Gunter prepared a reply.

Gunter paused to contemplate the appropriate answer. With a stick that still held the tacky remains of a marshmallow, Gunter played with a wood chip at the edge of the fire as he spoke. "I can't speak for any other doctor—only me." He paused again as he watched a small flame dance atop the wood chip. The burning chip held everyone's eye as he spoke to their ears. "I would imagine it's not unlike a pastor who buries members of the church, who are one's friends, even having to conduct the funeral for a family member."

Oh, my god, he is going to talk about Mom. Anya closed her eyes and prayed for strength. Gunter continued speaking, unaware of the anxiety Anya was experiencing.

"Certainly, there is a moment of lament, as well as questioning. Did the medical team or I do everything possible? Or worse, did we miss anything? Even when all the t's are crossed and i's dotted, the result is the same: the person is dead. There is a line from one of the early *M*A*S*H* episodes that I need to remind myself about from time to time. 'Rule number one is young men die, and rule number two is doctors can't change rule number one.' Unfortunately, that doesn't lessen the pain of losing a patient. Despite what doctors may think, we are not God."

Alice spoke up, "It's the God complex, right? We have a good friend who is a neurologist and is extremely good at what he does, and if—"

Before she could complete her thought, Chuck interrupted. "Are you talking about Dr. Olsen? Yes, he is talented and highly respected. A couple of years ago, he performed—"

"His name is not important." Alice's lips were tight as she spoke, and the wrinkles across her brow deepened.

Chuck's head dropped to his chest, and as apologetic as possible, he whispered, "You are so right. I am sorry. Continue."

After several deep breaths, Alice continued. "I really believe that if you asked our friend, and he was totally honest, he would say that he hasn't changed rule number one yet, but it's only a matter of time. If I am totally honest, I must confess, I want a doctor who has that attitude."

Pulling the marshmallow stick from the fire to extinguish the flame on the end, Gunter nodded several times as he replied to Alice. "I can appreciate your desire to have the best physician. Unfortunately," he stopped nodding and reached for a marshmallow, which he stabbed with the stick, "I have seen doctors who refuse to let nature take its course. They refuse to stop when it's clear the person is gone. Or they refuse to stop trying extreme measures when the next step should be hospice—preparation for the final stage of life." With his marshmallow golden brown, he sat back, pulled the sugary substance from the stick, popped it in his mouth, and let others pick up the conversation.

Shatz, fresh from participating in ethical discussions at college on this very topic, asked the $64,000 question. Who decides it is time to stop medical treatment? And based on what criteria? The patient, family members, doctors? In an age driven by litigation, no doctor wants to be accused of not trying everything to save a patient. But, aside from that always present threat, if a patient is unable to speak for themselves and doesn't have a living will, also known as an advance directive, who decides?

With the innocence only expressed by an eighteen-year-old, Dillon looked at his hands as he spoke. "I can't imagine holding life and death in my hands." To accentuate the unbelievable, he repeated the last three words, "in my hands."

Quad, sitting across from Dillon, nursing a bottle of beer, said, "I may not hold human life in my hands, but each spring, during the calving season, I am literally holding life and death in my bloody hands. There are times when I have to let one die that probably wouldn't survive anyway in order to save two others. It's never easy, but it must be done."

"You're not equating the life of a calf with the life of a person, are you?" Shatz wasted no time in challenging Quad.

Before Quad could respond, Dusty offered up, "What if the one life allowed to die was that of a person for the sake of two people?"

"Come on, Dad. That's not what he said."

"But that is what I am asking."

"I know where this is going. I know you."

"Tell me then. Where is this going?"

"If I, or anyone else, were to suggest that we save two people, you will add ages or professions to the three individuals."

"And so, you are suggesting that age or occupation should be taken into consideration when determining who lives and who dies?" Dusty's lips parted slightly as though he was about to smile. "For the sake of discussion, let's say one individual is five years old, and the other two persons are sixty and seventy. Would you save the five-year-old or the sixty- and seventy-year-olds? You can't save all three."

"My initial, motherly response is to say, the five-year-old." Alice's voice quivered with passion. "We live in a society that values youth and potential. The future is more important than the past."

"I don't necessarily disagree, but we have no idea what the five-year-old might become or do in the future. For all we know, in ten years, that five-year-old child might be a high school dropout or, worse yet, a school shooter." Brit didn't shy away from saying difficult things.

Alice responded, "Nor do we know what the sixty- and seventy-year-olds have done or will do with their remaining days."

Dusty offered more to the narrative he started. "The five-year-old suffers from a rare illness, the sixty-year-old is a gifted physician who has experience with the rare illness, and the seventy-year-old carries a gene that has the potential to provide a cure. Now what?"

Quad asked, "So what's your point, boss?"

Shatz spoke immediately. "His point is that there is no simple answer."

Gunter entered the conversation. "Maybe there is no right answer. We only fool ourselves into thinking that if we just parse the situation and analyze it long enough, we will discover the right answer. But, again, maybe there is no right answer."

"That sounds rather disheartening, hopeless, pessimistic." Dillon's cheeks were red with emotion as he spoke.

"If I didn't have hope, I would stop being a doctor this very second. If I didn't have hope, there would be no reason to take another breath. But having hope doesn't mean I dismiss the complexity of life. In fact, it's the complexities of life, it's because of questions like Dusty's, and it's your honesty, Dillon, to admit that you can't imagine holding life and death in your hands that gives me hope."

The air around the campfire was filled with smoke and smoke alone as Gunter's words burrowed deep into everyone's thoughts. It was Chuck who eventually filled the air with words. The words were those he wanted to share earlier, but the conversation took a sudden turn, and it no longer seemed appropriate to speak. With Gunter bringing back Dillon's words, the opportunity presented itself again. "It's not just doctors who hold life and death in their hands. Anya, isn't your work about life and death?"

Startled by hearing her name being spoken and feeling the need to respond, if for no other reason than being polite, she kept her reply short. "I never thought of it in that manner." To herself, she acknowledged that she never identified her work in terms of life and death and that she was holding a person's life in her hands. As a therapist, that image struck a chord of uneasiness. It sounded and felt like a boundary issue. Certainly, every therapist recognizes the seriousness of their labors, but to take responsibility for a client's existence is dangerous. That approach could result in all types of unethical consequences. She thought she understood what Chuck was attempting to say and that he was merely trying to be kind, but it's that type of thinking that can be dangerous for the client as well. They may not understand the boundaries. They may become angry and frustrated with the therapist when certain needs they expect to have met are not being addressed. Rather than explain to Chuck why she never thought of it in that manner, she said nothing else.

The notion of life and death took on a slightly different perspective when Shatz subtly shifted the discussion by posing a question concerning everyone's bucket list.

"Thinking about life and death and the things you want to accomplish before you die, what is the next thing on your bucket list?"

The conversation bounced around until Chuck shared one item from his list. "Climbing Mount Everest."

Just about everyone had a comment and opinion to share about climbing Everest. It was Dusty, once again, who provided a current, and as far as everyone knew, an accurate description of policy changes. The conversation expanded to include the effects on the body while attempting to make the climb.

The sheer depth and magnitude of the topic invited all voices to share stories, heard or read, concerning the adventures of scaling Mount Everest. As a result, no one recognized that they were describing and discussing the gory details of freezing to death and trying to conquer the geography of a mountain as they enjoyed the warmth of a fire surrounded by mountains. Similarly, debating the new policies being enforced by Nepal and the long lines of people sitting, waiting to move, no one recognized that Bobby moved and placed himself between Gunter and Anya.

The hushed tones employed by Bobby forced Gunter to lean closer to the cowboy's black hat to hear as he spoke.

"A year ago, my mother passed away."

"I'm sorry for your loss."

"Thank you. But what I was wondering was, have you encountered many cases of Alzheimer's during your career?"

Shaking his head, Gunter responded without stating a specific number of cases he encountered, yet made it clear that it was too many. "The progressive destruction of a person's memory and ability to think." He paused as he frowned and then continued. "I describe to family members that Alzheimer's is the robber that will steal your loved one's identity, leaving a shell that looks like your loved one."

"Boy, isn't that the truth." Bobby removed his hat and used his handkerchief to wipe sweat from his brow. Sweat dripped from the pores, not because it was hot, not because of physical labor, but because of emotional labor.

Gunter watched Bobby without staring directly at him and concluded that his palms were more than likely tacky, as emotional stress seeps from the palms of one's hands and forehead. The observation caused Gunter to ask, "So, how was it with your mom?"

"Difficult. She ended up in a memory care unit. In the end, she didn't really know anyone, at least not consistently. She knew me, but there would be times she didn't. She also identified me as my dad. I sort of looked like him when he was younger, and there would be times that she referred to me by my dad's name. What became more difficult was my siblings' inability to deal with Mom. To use your image, they couldn't get used to the shell of Mom."

"That's pretty common. Alzheimer's rips at the family structure."

Bobby nodded as he smiled and then said, "It was even worse for my family due to the fact that we were ripped apart before Alzheimer's made an appearance. What was painful to witness was that my siblings couldn't let Mom be who she was becoming."

"That's pretty profound, Bobby. I mean, that is insightful. Letting Mom be who she was becoming. Wow." Gunter nodded his head several times before concluding his thought. "If family members would do that, this journey might be just a bit less stressful. Not easier, it's never easy, but some of the anger and frustration might evaporate."

"I think what compounded the problem was, when it came time to let her go, they couldn't do it. There was too much-unresolved stuff. Unfortunately, Mom no longer had the mental facilities necessary to participate in resolving the past. She was present, she was there, but she wasn't present, she wasn't there. The Mom we all knew was gone.

"And at that point, life is more challenging for the family than it is for the individual with Alzheimer's. Once they reach that point, they no longer realize what they once knew. They no longer realize what they don't know."

Anya, who had been listening to the entire conversation, spoke for the first time. "It's like a death, yet the person never leaves."

Even though Bobby sat between Gunter and Anya, they made eye contact, and both fully knew that her words spoke volumes. Her words fit more contexts than just Bobby's, but it was Bobby who spoke.

"That's exactly how it felt. The woman we knew as Mom had died. She no longer existed, yet she did. We could visit her, sit with her, even have a meal with her, and yet never have our mother."

The three of them sat in silence, and Anya considered saying more but stopped herself as she understood that what she was contemplating was less about Alzheimer's and more about death and letting go. Eventually, Bobby stood and returned to the spot from which he came, and the three connected with the rest of the group. The night progressed as if that entire conversation never occurred. But it had occurred, and that couldn't be dismissed for any of the three.

Gunter hated to admit it, but like Henry, the main character in *Out of the Wild*, he wasn't one for talking about feelings and such things. Henry, like Gunter, lost his wife due to ill-fated actions. The major difference between the two, Gunter understood, as the character came to life in the pages, was that Henry threw himself into a bottle of booze while Gunter threw himself into work. Both options served the purpose of escaping feelings and such things. However, the latter was more socially acceptable, possibly making it more dangerous. The saving factor for Gunter was nestled deep in her sleeping bag, reading her book. Otherwise, he, too, would have lived his nights measuring the number of swigs left in the bottle.

Redemption, for Henry, came when he stopped trying to run away from himself and, thereby, stopped punishing himself. Gunter couldn't avoid the question: Was he punishing himself for Katharina's death? Even more disturbing, was Anya attempting to do the same thing? "It's like death, and yet she never leaves." And what about those words,

"And so have I." It was time to stop trying to escape. He needed to talk to his daughter.

"So, you, too, dream about Katharina?"

At the bedside of a patient or in the office, he didn't have any problem being forthright and honest. Words never escaped him. Skillfully, with the greatest of empathy, he could deliver the most tragic news and then invite the individual or the family to consider the next steps. More times than he cared to count, it was his responsibility to inform family members that their loved one passed away. With compassion and sensitivity, he knew not only what to say but when to say it. With Anya, it was entirely different.

Words eluded him when he needed to say the right thing. It didn't matter how many times he practiced. It didn't matter the size of the word bank he created or the quality of the words deposited; when it was time for a withdrawal, the account was empty. It baffled him that the person he loved the most was the most difficult person with whom to speak. It wasn't anything Anya did or didn't do. It was all about him.

Over the years, on various occasions, he tried to determine the first time he struggled to speak honestly and openly with Anya. The hope was simple. If he could identify when that started, he might be able to reverse it. Even better, he could explain to his daughter why, all these years, he struggled to broach difficult topics with her. His efforts were futile, until that afternoon. Seeing the elk face down in the water transported him back in time.

It was a hot July afternoon. For the past month, Anya had been pestering Gunter to purchase an inflatable pool. Commercials, strategically placed during cartoons, were advertising inflatable pools. The perfect gift, the ideal thing to have on a hot summer afternoon. Of course, the selection of pools was endless. There were one-ring pools, two and three rings, molded pools, pools barely large enough for an infant, and pools that could hold a family of eight. Fortunately, the commercials persuaded Anya that there was only one acceptable pool for their backyard. The pool that caught the five-year-old's eye was a Smurf pool.

So, it was on a hot Saturday afternoon in July, while Anya was staying at Grandpa and Grandma's house, that Gunter purchased a Smurf pool. When she returned home and saw the pool, she immediately replaced her clothes with a swimsuit and informed Gunter he needed to do the same.

With Anya splashing about in the Smurf pool and Gunter comfortably seated in a lawn chair with his feet in the water, the two covered the highlights of Anya's stay with her grandparents. It had been three days, and she had a lot to describe. Gunter, with a beer in hand, listened intently and probed for details at the appropriate times. As the stories seemed to wind down, he asked, "It sounds like you had a good time. Would you like to stay longer next time?"

"Yes, but I like to come home." The next set of words nearly drowned Gunter in the Smurf pool, or at least, it felt like he was drowning. "When is Mommy coming home?"

Anya had never inquired about Katharina coming home or being at home. Without a prompt, as a five-year-old, she seldom asked about her mother. Gunter initiated the conversations concerning Katharina and usually focused on one of the pictures of Katharina displayed throughout the house. This was the first time Anya initiated any discussion concerning her mommy.

Carefully, Gunter tried to determine why she was asking about Mommy coming home. What, if anything, was the source of this question? Confident that he had not said anything that might solicit such a question, he inquired further about the three days spent with Grandpa and Grandma. The informal questions revealed that Rex, a three-year-old collie, had been missing for a day and a half. Grandpa assured Anya that there was nothing to worry about. He was just out hunting. According to Anya, Grandpa said, "He will return. He loves us, and this is his home."

When Rex finally showed up, Grandpa again said, "See, he came home because he loves us."

Gunter felt ambushed by his father. He wanted to pick up the phone and call his father and shout, "What were you thinking? How could you say those things to Anya?"

Instead, he needed to respond to his daughter, who had asked a second time about Mommy returning. It made logical sense. He had assured Anya that Mommy loved her very much. And, of course, based on her experience with Rex, anyone who loves you returns home.

Beads of sweat rolled down his sides. The lawn chair was slimy from the perspiration that formed in the middle of his back. He considered sliding into the pool and possibly distracting Anya, but that wasn't fair to Anya. Instead, he leaned forward and said, "You remember how I told you that Mommy is in heaven?"

"Oh," was all she said. She turned her attention back to Barbie and Ken, who floated atop the water.

He leaned back against the damp chair and breathed a huge sigh of relief. Tipping the bottle upright, he drained the remainder of the amber liquid and felt confident that he addressed her question without having to explain death to a five-year-old. Before the thick glass bottom of the bottle pressed the blades of grass downward, Anya offered an alternative.

Without removing her gaze from the dolls, she said, "Let's go to heaven and see Mommy."

The ease at which she made the suggestion told Gunter that for Anya, going to heaven was just like going to Grandpa and Grandma's for a visit. His dilemma just got worse. Now he had to explain why Mommy wasn't coming home and why they couldn't go visit her in heaven.

He tried one more time to answer her request without unpacking the entire issue. "Someday, we will go to heaven and visit Mommy, but right now, you are swimming in your new pool."

"Okay. Tomorrow we can go."

Gunter felt horrible that he was so unprepared and ill-equipped to address his own daughter's questions. He wanted to pray that come tomorrow she would forget, but he knew better. Anya was not one to forget. He had five years to prepare for this moment. Why had he continued to put it off? He knew that someday his stories about Katharina would invoke questions, but …

"So, you, too, dream about Katharina?" This time, the words escaped from his body and laid heavy upon him until they reached Anya's ears. He needed her. He needed her to carry part of the load. He needed her to validate his efforts. He needed her to be patient. He needed his daughter to forgive him despite his flaws and his failures.

She reciprocated, "Yeah, just about every night." Even though she didn't name it for herself, at that moment, she knew what she needed. She needed him to listen. She needed him to be open. She needed him to accept her. She needed her father to forgive her despite her guilt and failures.

They needed each other, yet they were both silent. Neither one was quite sure what to say next, so they said nothing. Silence wasn't anything new for them, nor was it any longer deemed negative. That hadn't always been the case. There was a time when both Gunter and Anya wanted to shout, "SAY SOMETHING!" The song "Say Something, I'm Giving Up on You," sung by A Great Big World and Christina Aguilera, captured their life for a period.

Every individual goes through a period when they struggle to become mature in thought and deeds, struggle to determine what is important, struggle to unearth what they value, and struggle to implement the values that will inform their choices. Anya was no different. If anything, her struggle might have been a bit greater than some.

Two days after her tenth birthday, Anya attended her second funeral. The first, she didn't remember, being only days old. The second pried open Pandora's Box, the lid of which couldn't be closed, unlike the cover of Grandma's casket.

After Susan's departure, Anya's grandma, Hildy, was the woman whom she drifted toward to be the mom figure. Hildy was the person who could tell the stories of Katharina's childhood and how Anya was just like her mom. She also played the role of offering motherly advice and criticism. Gunter's mom, equally important in Anya's life, fulfilled the role of grandma. The one to spoil her.

News of Hildy's death came unexpectedly. She was driving home from an afternoon of quilting at the church when a drunk driver crossed the center line a hundred feet in front of her car. Hildy never had a chance to swerve to avoid the collision. The police report stated that she died at the scene. The coroner's report read, "Hildy died on impact." As is often the case, the twenty-year-old drunk driver walked away from the accident with a broken arm and a few minor cuts.

Martin, Anya's grandpa, asked the police if they would notify Gunter of Hildy's death. After receiving the news, Gunter, at the end of the school day, picked his daughter up at Kennedy Elementary School.

"Hi, Dad. Is this an early birthday surprise?"

"Not really."

"What's the occasion? You never get off work in time to pick me up."

"I thought we could stop by the beach."

"In May? Kinda cold for a swim, Dad. Don't you remember, there were snowflakes just two weeks ago?"

While skipping smooth rocks across the top of the water, Gunter eventually found the words to tell Anya of the tragic event. Holding a perfectly round rock in her hand, she listened as Gunter knelt next to her and shared the news that Grandma was in a terrible accident and didn't survive. She stepped in close to him and tucked her head against his chest. Together they wept. They wept for Hildy, they wept for Martin, and they wept for each other.

Feeling the rhythm of Anya's breathing reminded Gunter of how, during the days and weeks following her birth, he carried her close to his chest, and without ever looking, he knew from the pattern of her breathing if she was awake or asleep.

Straightening up, she opened her hand, revealing the smooth rock, and said, "I'm going to skip this rock for Grandma."

Gunter smiled and said, "She'd like that." He was surprised, and yet, he wasn't.

Anya continued to do and say the unexpected.

Two days after her birthday, Anya found herself positioned between her grandpa and her dad and two strides behind the casket as it was carried to the front of the church. Holding each of their hands, she marched them down the aisle. At times, she felt her grandpa's right hand tighten and pull back as though preparing to refuse to go any farther. On each occasion, she looked up at him with her big brown eyes and softly squeezed his hand as though saying, "It's okay, Grandpa. I'm still here."

During the internment, as people gathered around a hole, waiting for the casket to be lowered into the dust of the earth, Anya kept one hand tightly clenched. She sat quietly and listened to every word the pastor said. After the pastor said, "We commit Hildy's body to its resting place, earth to earth, ashes to ashes, and dust to dust," her free hand tugged on Gunter's shirt sleeve.

As he leaned toward his daughter, he heard her say, "I brought a smooth rock. Can I leave it with Grandma?" Unable to form any words, as his throat swelled shut and tears flowed, he nodded and pointed to the casket. Sliding past the pastor, Anya stood next to the casket, carefully stretched out her arm, and placed the smooth, brown rock atop Hildy's casket.

Of those assembled at the graveside, the only face not wet was Anya's. When she returned to her seat, she took hold of Grandpa's hand and whispered, "Now Grandma and Mommy can skip rocks together in heaven."

In the weeks that followed, Anya avoided conversations with her dad. When she did speak, her demonstrative mannerism was absent. Mealtimes, which previously bubbled with energy as she recounted every minute of her day, were hauntingly still. She was barely visible around the house. Her room became her asylum. Television, including her favorite shows like *Full House* and *Friends*, couldn't lure her into the living room. Gunter's attempts to communicate only seemed to make matters worse.

Anger that seldom made an appearance resided just below the surface, waiting to fester and pop through the pores of her existence. The unpredictability of her mood swings made life in the house challenging. Recognizing the signs of depression, Gunter scheduled an appointment for Anya to meet with a therapist.

After the third appointment, the therapist, Dr. Natalie Post, summoned Gunter for a meeting. The purpose of the meeting was to share her clinical diagnosis and a plan for moving forward.

"Anya," Dr. Post began, "is a mature, exceptionally gifted young lady. I haven't met many, if any, ten-year-olds who have her vocabulary and are able to reason as she does. As positive as these things are, they are also an Achilles' heel."

Gunter frowned and cocked his head to the left as he spoke. "I'm not sure I follow."

"In my professional opinion, two different things are going on here for your daughter, which are interrelated. The most recent trigger, for both, was the death of her grandmother."

Gunter nodded in agreement. He didn't doubt that Hildy's death was the source of his daughter's behavioral changes. What wasn't clear in his mind was how Anya's giftedness was problematic. But rather than bark out an objection, he sat quietly and waited for Dr. Post to offer clarity. It was called professional courtesy.

"One of the reasons for the silence is due to the fact that there is no one to mediate between the two of you. There is no one to redirect you in the midst of a heated discussion. There is no one to reassure Anya that you love her in the midst of a disagreement. There is no one else, for either of you, to be angry with. And unfortunately, the one you need to perform that role is the one who is the source of the problem. Anya's grandmother was the closest person she had to play that role. With her now gone, it's too risky for Anya to put herself out there."

Gunter wanted to defend himself. He wanted to say, "Look, Doc, you think I don't already know this? Of course, none of this would be happening if Katharina was here, but she's not, nor will she ever be. So, tell me something I don't know. Something that will help Anya."

"The other thing is that your daughter doesn't know how to express her grief. She's scared."

"Scared? Scared of what?"

Before answering, Dr. Post scanned her notes. She flipped through several yellow legal pad pages. "At this point, I'm not sure. I could guess, but that's all it would be. We need to spend more time together."

"What is your suggestion?"

"Unfortunately, unlike the patients you see, I can't prescribe a pill or a procedure that will fix her or address the problem. Be patient. Give her space to work through these issues and try to avoid heated discussions."

Gunter was now totally confused. The woman seated across from him continued to bring up the notion that he and Anya were engaged in heated discussions. The truth was, he avoided such confrontations at all costs. The problem was there were no discussions. He needed clarity.

"I am a bit confused. Did Anya say that we have heated discussions?"

"No, not exactly."

"Did she hint at this?"

"Well, no."

Rubbing his chin, he paused before he continued to question. "Tell me, why then have you continued to imply that we have heated discussions?"

"Don't you?"

"Ah, no!"

"Really?"

"Really! It is the absence of conversation that has me concerned. You see, I'm the one who tends to avoid conversations that require vulnerability. It has always been Anya who pesters for honesty and the sharing of feelings. But that's all ceased since Hildy's funeral."

"I see."

Gunter, again, held his tongue, but he seriously wondered if Dr. Post understood.

Instead, he returned to her diagnosis. "I do fully agree. There is no one present to mediate our conversations. And the one needed to fulfill this role isn't going to make an appearance. I do agree. In fact, I have been concerned for some time now that Anya doesn't know how to express her grief. Her feelings and her passions are so deep that it scares me that she's stopped sharing anything and everything. It scares me to hear you say, 'She's scared.' Quite honestly, that's why I brought her to you."

Gunter placed his trust in Dr. Post that with time she'd be able to help Anya work through her feelings. He trusted that as a skilled professional, she'd know how to proceed and that, over time, Anya would be able to express her grief. Therefore, it was difficult, for the next four years, to continually hear Anya describe her hatred for Dr. Post. Initially, he thought it wasn't necessarily a bad thing that Dr. Post pushed Anya to address things that made her uncomfortable. But as the years marched on, it never changed. Until finally, on her fourteenth birthday, Anya announced, "I am not going to therapy any longer."

Eventually, Gunter forgot about Anya's therapy sessions until she graduated from graduate school, when she stated, "You know, Dad, Dr. Post was part of my motivation to become an art therapist."

The words from ten years earlier streamed into his thoughts as he recalled his daughter's expressed hatred for Dr. Post. "I thought you hated her. Has your opinion of Dr. Post changed?"

"I did. I swore I would become a better therapist, or at least one who knows how to work with kids. She didn't have a clue."

On the eve of Anya's sixteenth birthday, a single hour short of sixteen years since

Katharina passed away, Gunter, having finished reviewing the records of his patients scheduled for their next day appointments, heard Anya crying as he drew close to her room. With his hand on the doorknob, Gunter stopped himself. He wanted to rush in and scoop up his baby, but she wasn't a baby anymore. She was now on the brink of adulthood. He also didn't want to interrupt whatever emotion was spilling forth, as this was the first time he heard her cry since the day he shared the news of Hildy's death.

Lifting his hand from the knob, he had to admit that it wasn't only his concern for Anya that stopped him from entering her room but also his insecurities. He was afraid if he passed through the door, he would not be able to control his own emotions. Like a dam breaking, he feared that the flood of his own tears would consume them both. Rather than imposing upon her personal space, Gunter slid to the floor in the hallway, closed his eyes, and just listened.

At the breakfast table, adorned with a balloon bearing the words *Sweet Sixteen*, accompanied by a dozen roses, and her favorite breakfast food, waffles smothered in whipped cream, strawberries, and chocolate, Gunter awaited Anya's arrival, not sure what to expect.

Silence didn't invade the space on the other side of Anya's door until well after one o'clock in the morning.

"Good morning, Dad. Is all this for me?" Anya greeted him.

"Well, it's not my sixteenth birthday, so I guess it must be for you. Happy birthday!"

"Thanks, Dad. You are going to sing, right?"

Gunter paused. He couldn't remember the last time she asked him to sing. There was a different air about his daughter. The heaviness of the past several years seemed to have evaporated. Her smile appeared authentic. Even her voice had an octave he had not heard for a long, long time.

"Yeah, I'll sing."

The lyrics, "*Happy birthday to you. Happy birthday to you,*" and the tune bounced in his thoughts when Anya broke the silence and brought him back to the tent. "When you dream about Mom, what do you dream?"

He started this. Now he had to follow through and tell the truth. Avoidance was no longer an option. He closed his eyes for a moment to behold the beauty of the woman who comes to him in his dreams. The woman who brings a smile to his face, who causes his insides to stir with excitement, who invites him to be still and just be. He cleared his throat and then spoke. "I dream about you. Your mom alw—"

"Wait, what did you just say?" Accompanying her words and to express her confusion, she lifted her shoulders from the air mattress, twisted her torso toward him, and rested on her left forearm as she added, "And don't go trying to evade the question." She needed him to be honest with her.

"No, no." He even waved his hands as though surrendering. "I am being totally honest."

"Right." She laughed as her head shook. "I ask about Mom and what you dream, and you say 'me.'"

Patting the air, Gunter makes a plea for patience. "Just wait. Just—just be patient and let me finish, and you will see that my answer is the truth." He didn't wait for her to respond. With haste, he proceeded.

"Regardless of the setting, regardless the time of year, for that matter, regardless of the specific date, for the past thirty-eight years, your mom arrives wearing the same thing, and she never ages. Your mom looks as she did on our wedding day: youthful, angelic, gorgeous, exquisitely stunning. The glow that radiated from her was contagious. The same glow precedes her arrival. But contrary to what you might expect, she's not adorned in her wedding gown."

"What is she," Anya pauses, "wearing?"

"She is wearing a navy floral dress."

"And, what's the significance of a navy floral dress?"

"It's the dress I purchased for—" Gunter realized that he had never discussed her mother's funeral with his daughter.

The interlude was greater than Anya could tolerate, so she delivered his words back to him so that he might complete the sentence. "You were saying, the dress you purchased, for what?"

"I'm sorry, I just realized something else." He shook his head as though he was an Etch A Sketch and could wipe away any thought. "Your mom arrives wearing the dress I purchased for her funeral."

Anya took a moment to consider the complexity of that vision. "That's rather interesting, Dad. Mom comes as, what, a twenty-four-year-old wearing the last item of clothing you ever saw on her?"

"Exactly, and you know what? It took me years to actually recognize that."

"What do you think it means?"

He shrugged his shoulders. "I honestly don't have any idea."

Rather than getting bogged down, at this stage, in interpreting the dreams, she attempted to keep things moving forward. "So, where am I in these dreams?"

"It's really simple. You are the focal point of every visit. Now, this might sound a bit weird."

"These are dreams, Dad. There is no such thing as weird, because there is no norm. For something to be labeled as weird, it has to go against or challenge the expected behavior or norm."

"Whoa. Who's getting philosophical now?"

"Hey, it's bound to happen sooner or later, after all the years of being on the receiving end."

The brief hiatus allowed for some of the pressure to be released before Gunter continued. Humor, when employed correctly, is like opening a valve in an over-inflated situation.

"As I was saying, when your mom appears in my dreams, we discuss you."

"What do you mean, you discuss me?" Anya sounded more defensive than she intended.

"We talk about you. We have from the very beginning. The conversations might have been about something you were struggling with or something I struggled with in my relationship with you. It didn't matter what the context was. Every visit focused on you."

She took a deep breath before she asked the next question. "Why do you think that is?"

"I don't know. Maybe, maybe I need your mom to help me be a parent."

"Yeah, I suppose that makes sense. Maybe you also thought it wasn't fair that she didn't get to parent me, and so you, I don't know, create that opportunity for her to do that."

"So, you're suggesting that this was more about her than me?"

"No. This is about you, Dad. They're your dreams. It's just another way for you to look at yourself and Mom."

"That's possible. But I always feel better after our visits."

"Always?"

"You know what I mean. There literally were times when I received an answer to a question or a concern I had." Gunter paused as though considering an answer he received. He continued without explaining the silence. "I don't know how I would have parented without your mom visiting me." He raised both hands and added, "I know how that sounds, but—" He couldn't say anything else.

Reaching over, Anya touched his shoulder and said, "Dad, you did just fine being my dad."

"Yeah, well," he stopped to find the right words to express what he was thinking and feeling. Once again, his word bank was empty.

"Do you remember what Bobby said?"

"Excuse me? I need some context here. I'm not following you."

"Tonight, when he was speaking about his mom, I'm just wondering if something he said might fit."

"Which was?"

"You even commented on the profoundness of his thought."

"Oh, yeah. Letting his mom be who she was becoming. Your point here?"

"I am wondering if that might apply to us?"

Gunter repeated the words, this time slower, emphasizing each word. "Letting Mom be who she was becoming." Gunter looked directly at Anya as he asked her, "What about your dreams? What do you dream?"

Anya rolled back on the air mattress and breathed deeply before sharing. "I don't remember the first time I dreamed about Mom. I do remember, even as a young child, feeling the height of her touch."

Gunter smiled as he listened to the descriptions of the various ways in which Katharina would place a hand upon Anya. She ended the narrative by pondering why every visit included some form of physical contact.

"I have never told you this. It never seemed like something important to share. The night you were born, after the nurses cleaned up your mom, you and I had several minutes alone with her. It was an opportunity for us to be a family. I carefully placed you in the nave of her arm. I remember thinking, *I can't give you the sound of her voice, but I can give you her touch.*"

"I just felt a shiver race through my body."

"It was the first time since they had placed you in my arms that you were still. Prior to that, your tiny arms were in continuous movement, and your legs would kick against the blanket. But there, against your mom's side, cradled by her arm, you were at rest." Gunter gave Anya space to absorb her past, a past she didn't know about until that moment.

He eventually spoke. "I am curious. What does your mom look like when she appears in your dreams? And if she speaks, how does she sound?"

"Sound?"

"When your mom spoke, literally, people would stop and listen. There was something about her voice that was pleasing to the ear. It resulted in tranquility."

"Tranquility? Can't say I have ever heard a voice I would describe as tranquil. Maybe the closest would be Morgan Freeman. But Mom didn't sound like Morgan Freeman, did she?"

"No." Gunter laughed. "Although her tone was husky, sultry, she did have the same rhythm as Mr. Freeman. That's what it was." Excitement raised the pitch of Gunter's voice. "There was a rhythm to the words she spoke. Like the waves of an ocean lapping up on the beach, her voice was peaceful and calming."

Anya, again, leaned on her forearm, driving her chest away from the mattress. Facing Gunter, she said, "Now that you mention Mom's voice, I can't describe what she sounds like. I guess I never really thought about it, but—" She stopped speaking as though trying to hear her mom's voice in her head. After a few seconds, she shook her head and said, "I can't describe it." The weight of the revelation drove her back onto the air mattress. Speaking to herself, she added, "I can't believe I never thought about her voice."

"Why would you? It was a dream."

"I suppose, but I do remember identifying that she always arrived wearing the same outfit."

"Oh yeah? What outfit?"

"You remember the picture of Mom that sat on your dresser?"

"Um, you might need to be more specific. Over the years there have been more than one."

"The one that sat in the middle and was there for years."

"Is it a college picture?"

"I don't know. I never heard the story behind that picture. Mom was standing on the edge of the ocean. I assumed it was the ocean, with the waves washing up to her knees, and she was wearing a white swimsuit covering?"

"Oh, yeah. I love that picture. It was spring break of our senior year. We didn't have any money, but somehow, we managed to get to South Padre Island. We slept in the car or on the beach when the nights were warm. That picture was taken mid-morning. Not warm enough to go swimming but too warm for more clothes than a swimsuit. It was our last day before heading back to the snow and cold."

"When you look at the picture, you can't tell if Mom was putting on the white crochet swimsuit cover-up or taking it off. Her hands playfully are holding the ties as though she was teasing you."

"That was exactly what she was doing. It was a side of your mom she seldom displayed in public." Gunter took a deep breath, savoring the image of which Anya reminded him. "I never realized you paid much attention to that picture."

"I often wondered why, when you selected pictures to talk about

Mom, you never selected that one."

"I guess you're right. I never did. I don't think it was a conscious decision on my part." Gunter stopped himself from sharing anything else. The truth was Katharina was walking toward him when he snapped that picture. She was in the process of removing the cover-up. When she drew close, she reached up and kissed him softly, and together they found the beach blanket. There, beneath the sun-filled sky, with the gulf water washing their toes, they made love for the very first time.

The picture belonged in the bedroom, the very room where Gunter and Katharina conceived Anya. Gunter smiled as he considered how ironic it was that Katharina would visit Anya, in her dreams, wearing the white crochet cover-up. The smile was short-lived as he once again concluded that not only did the picture belong in the bedroom, but the very image of Katharina belonged in a frame and not in Anya's dreams, night after night. A single tear escaped from the corner of his eye as he acknowledged that the same conclusion held true for him. The image of Katharina in the navy floral dress belonged in a casket and not in his dreams.

Chapter 8

Gunter woke to the sound of voices, which was unusual, as each morning, he was the first to step out of the tent. Equally startling was the fact that he didn't need to use his headlamp to see the hands on his watch; the sun was already at work. The faded glow-in-the-dark hands revealed it was three minutes after seven. He couldn't remember the last time he slept past six, and that was considered late. The voices belonged to Jack and Bobby, and they were loud enough that Anya stirred.

With breakfast in less than an hour, Gunter felt it was an acceptable time to speak with Anya. "Good morning, sunshine."

With a partial yawn and stretch that drove her arms out of the sleeping bag and past her head, she asked, "What time is it?" Acknowledging the time, she said, "Dad, I could have slept for another thirty-five minutes and still made breakfast."

"Sorry."

"No, that's okay. I can't believe how refreshed I feel this early."

"You know, I can't believe I slept this late."

Unrehearsed, and yet in unison, they both asked, "Did you—" Hearing the other, they both stopped.

Gunter spoke first. "Go ahead."

"No, you go ahead and finish." Anya's smile consumed her face as she added, "Age before beauty."

Not to be outdone, Gunter asked, "What if I have both?"

"Now you're just being silly."

They both laughed, and Gunter finished his question. "Did you dream about Mom?"

Without answering, Anya stated, "That was my question, too." Rather than speaking, both simply shook their head, no.

After a tummy-filling breakfast that included freshly baked blueberry muffins, Dusty described the options for the day.

"There is a fabulous trout stream about an hour's ride from camp. Even if the trout aren't biting, which I have never experienced, the scenery is spectacular."

Chuck spoke up immediately, "I'm not sure I am ready for an hour-and-a-half to two-hour horse ride." He didn't need to say anything else. Everyone knew what he was implying. More to the point, it didn't seem as amusing or witty in the morning as it did in the evening around the campfire.

With the same unguarded and defenseless manner as consistently displayed, Dusty continued with the description of options. "There are several hiking trails that lead out of camp. One trail will actually meet up with the trout stream." He held up a finger as he detailed the trail. "That hike is long and challenging, but the trail is good. As always, one can stay in camp and relax, sleep, or do whatever you want."

Jack and Bobby spoke up first. "We plan to go fishing."

Jack added, "If it's the stream I fished the last time I was here, Dusty's right; the trout are just waiting to feed upon our flies."

Gunter looked at Anya as he spoke. "We didn't purchase an out-of-state license just to frame it. We're in."

Alice, who stood beside her husband with her arm wrapped around his, spoke softly, "My knee is feeling much better. I would like to go for a hike. Not the strenuous trail, but a good hike. Something that gets the blood flowing." When Chuck didn't say anything, she turned and looked him squarely in the eye.

He spoke to her, but everyone could hear. "I wasn't sure if you wanted me along or if you just wanted some 'me' time out on the trail."

"Of course, I want you along. Why am I standing next to you?"

Addressing Dusty, wearing a smile, Chuck said, "I'm going hiking."

The group, in turn, embellished a smile, and Dusty, dry as dust, responded, "Okay then."

The six of them left on horseback, Dusty in the lead and Dillon bringing up the rear, ponying a mule. Once it was determined who was doing what, Brit quickly volunteered to accompany Alice and Chuck on their hike since this was her first visit to the campsite.

Quad, in need of rest, offered to stay in camp, while Shatz shared that after shuffling through her flashcards, she would more than likely hike down to the trout stream. That left Dillon with the task of packing up his fishing gear as he would serve as a fishing guide. A duty that only extended his smile further and fueled his adolescent enthusiasm for life.

After five days in the wilderness, Anya didn't expect that the words *remote*, *secluded*, *isolated*, *uninhabited*, and *desolate* would continue to define the scenery. She truly was in awe of the beauty and grandeur, which led to the realization that words like *remote* and *uninhabited* don't have to be associated with negative images. What captured her attention, as the six of them rode down the trail, was that in the middle of the wilderness, it appeared that they were even more remote, as though they were entering a space that was untouched by human hands. The isolation was augmented by the fact that other than horses' hooves and occasional *toots* from the back end of the horses, as they labored up and down the mountain, humans and animals traveled in silence. It was a silence that enabled Gunter's comment from the night before to endlessly roll through her thoughts.

Bobby and Dillon, who followed her petite gelding, were unaware of her consternation as Anya sat square and graceful in the saddle. And yet—

Gunter's words caught her off guard as the two of them had shared some very personal thoughts. They both were working at being honest with each other and being honest with themselves. Perhaps he was being more honest than she was prepared to hear when he said, "I wonder, I wonder if our relationship could be defined as the continental divide. We seem to be at the same place, standing on the same pinnacle of life, and yet," the *and yet* was painful for Anya to hear over and over, "and yet, so often we have been on two different sides of life. At times, flowing in two different directions."

Anya's horse must have sensed what the humans who surrounded her did not—the heaviness within her heart and head—for not once did he lower his head to snatch a bit of grass, not once did he push his nose into the butt of Jack's horse, not once did he drift to the edge of the path. Instead, his pace was smooth and uncomplicated, inviting Anya to ponder the heaviness within her body and spirit. It's a gift that horses possess: the ability to read the hearts and minds of humans. It's a gift that makes them exceptional therapists. It's a gift of nature that ensures their survival. The gift, by some, has been defined as a fight-or-flight instinct. In the wild, that instinct is critical. In domesticated settings, the gift maintains balance within the herd and with humans. In domesticated settings, the gift also offers humans the opportunity to experience balance and wholeness in ways that may be amiss.

The rhythm of the horse's footfall regulated her breathing and freed her mind to travel beyond the Bob Marshall Wilderness, beyond the wilderness of isolation, beyond the wilderness of the moment, to a multitude of times when she stood on the Continental Divide struggling to determine which way her life would flow.

"I need to make happy." With both feet firmly planted on the second step of a three-step stool, Anya leaned forward with her hands resting on the sink as she stared at her reflection. Despite the tears, despite the upper lip that quivered, the tiny face of a six-year-old tried to push the corners of her mouth toward her ears. The words she heard in her head were, "I need to make happy." Yet the frustrating fact for the girl who looked out from the mirror was that the more she forced the corners of her mouth, the greater the number of tears that escaped from the corners of her eyes. She eventually gave up trying to count the droplets as they molded into a stream.

"I need to make happy." She carefully watched as her mouth moved as she spoke the words aloud. She thought to herself, *Perhaps if I watch my mouth as I say the word "happy," I will know how to make my face happy.* But her face didn't resemble happy. She began to panic as it was only a matter of time before Gunter would summon her to the breakfast table.

She tried another word. "Smile." The results were the same. The corners of her mouth did not push upward. Word after word was spoken into the mirror in hopes of making a happy face. Despite uttering words that aligned with being happy, not a single word created a face of happy.

Marching into the kitchen, where the table was filled with presents and, of course, her favorite breakfast, waffles covered with whipped cream, strawberries, and chocolate, she continued to mumble, "I need to make happy. I need to make happy."

"What did you say, honey?"

"Oh, nothing. Just a silly rhyme."

"Happy birthday." Gunter, not known for his singing ability, launched into singing, "Happy Birthday."

Anya tried her best to smile, to make happy, all the while saying to herself, *Birth day sucks! How does one celebrate their birthday when that day was your mom's death day?*

Dusty turned back in his saddle as his horse continued down the trail. He instructed Dillon with a wave of his hand to take the trail to the right. In less than a tenth of a mile, the trail would reconnect with the main trail, and Dillon, along with the ponied mule, would pull in directly behind Dusty.

Dusty used the opportunity to offer an update before settling back into his saddle. "In about twenty minutes, we'll hit the spot where Dillon, Gunter, and Anya can turn down toward the stream while we travel on farther." A single flick of his pointer finger implied the additional travel was at least another fifteen or twenty minutes beyond the point of separation.

As Anya watched Dillon move ahead of the group, birth day was all she could think about. The challenge of "I need to make happy" didn't end the year her birth day arrived, and she wasn't with Gunter. She still tried to lift the corners of her mouth, because everyone's supposed to be happy on the day that marks their birth. The worst birth day occurred in 2010.

"Happy birthday to you. Happy birthday to you." Out of tune, Gunter sang for Anya.

"Dad, it's—it's dark outside." Lowering her phone to read the time, Anya shouted, "Dad! It's five o'clock in the morning."

"I know. Sorry about that. I have a busy day, and I assumed you would be celebrating after work since it's a Friday. I didn't want to miss wishing you a happy birthday."

"Thanks, Dad."

"Do you have plans for the evening?"

"Yeah, a couple of my friends from grad school and a handful of people from work have been planning a night out on the town. I told them it's just another birthday. It's not a landmark date, but once they discovered I was turning twenty-eight on the twenty-eighth, they made a big deal about it being my golden birthday."

"Any idea what the plans are?"

"No, they just keep telling me not to have any plans for Saturday because I won't be in any shape to do anything."

"Well, whatever it is, have fun, but be safe."

"Yes, Dad."

"Oh, yeah, I mailed your birthday card to your work, and there's a little something in there for you. Don't spend it all in one place."

"Thanks, Dad. It's unfortunate that we can't trust the mail delivery system here in Chicago. Any envelopes containing money or checks go missing."

"You do know that if you lived in Minnesota, that sort of thing would never happen."

Anya didn't need to see her dad's face to know he was grinning from ear to ear. "I think I have heard that before from someone."

"Get used to it. You'll hear it again. Hey, I gotta get going here. You be safe, and again, happy birthday. I love you."

"Love you too, Dad. Thanks for calling."

Dropping the phone atop the covers, Anya found herself unable to fall back asleep as the words *golden birthday* haunted her. She discovered herself thinking, *I need to make happy. People have gone to great lengths to make this a celebration, a festive occasion. I need to make happy. But how? What's golden about this birthday? This day is more horrible than the other twenty-seven.*

Seventeen hours after speaking with her dad, Anya was holding her own. No one would have guessed that if given a choice, she would have preferred to stay in bed all day and pretend the day never occurred. She laughed at the gifts that contained subtle and not-so-subtle sexual innuendos. She blushed, yet thanked everyone, as the group invited the entire bar to sing "Happy Birthday." She genuinely appreciated her friends and their determination to make this birthday, her golden birthday, the best. She was holding her own until the fourth boilermaker was set before her.

The alcohol was attacking her defenses meant to keep her from focusing on May 28, her birth day, as well as death day. The smile started to fade, and the laughter was replaced by silence. Rather than facing the crowd, as she had done for the past three hours, her barstool swiveled toward the wooden countertop, and she stared at the slender beer glass that held a whisky shot. The party continued without her. Few in the bar even noticed as the alcohol killed the brain cells that enabled social recognition.

Startled, Anya felt the weight of a hand on her shoulder. Lifting her head and looking in the mirror, behind the enormous display of liquor bottles, she saw her boss. Turning sideways, her boss slid in next to Anya while trying to ignore the intoxicated lush on the barstool behind her, whose hands groped her ass.

In the soft voice that she always used, no matter the situation, Anya's boss asked, "Are you okay?"

Slurring her words slightly, she answered, "Yeah, I've just had a lot to drink tonight."

"Tell me something I don't already know. I think I know you pretty well, sister.

There's something else bothering you. I've seen you drink before, but I have never seen you quite like this. What is it? You afraid of getting old?" She rested her hand on Anya's forearm and added with a smile, "Careful, I have a good twenty years on you."

"No. If only that was the issue. Every birth day—" she paused even longer than usual to execrate the separation with the hope that her boss might discern her intention. She concluded, "I have tried to make happy."

"Make happy?" Shaking her head, she added, "I don't understand."

"Right, few people do understand. I don't blame you. Birthdays are supposed to be happy occasions. A day every kid and every person looks forward to celebrating. Every kid, that is, but me."

"Okay, I guess." Perplexed, Anya's boss stopped herself before she said something stupid that would make the situation worse. She took a sip of her drink and informed the lush behind her to kindly remove his hand from her ass, or she'd remove it from his arm. Focusing back on Anya, she waited for the beer glass to strike the countertop before she leaned in and whispered, "Honey, I need more."

Continuing to stare at the mirror, Anya rattled off, "May 28, 1982."

"Your birthday."

"My birth day and my mom's death day."

Total confusion washed over her face. After several moments of silence, she said, "I—I don't understand, Anya. What are you saying?"

"My mom died giving birth to me."

"I am so sorry."

"Not only is today my golden birth day, but today is also a reminder that by turning twenty-eight, I am now officially older than when she died."

Without an attempt to offer shallow words of comfort, she placed her arms around Anya and held her tight. Anya melted into her boss's arms.

Sunday afternoon at two o'clock, her phone chirped, announcing that Gunter was calling to chat. She found herself uneasy and nervous when he inquired about how the celebration went. He informed her that he purposely refrained from calling on Saturday, assuming she would be in no shape to chat. For that, she was thankful. The truth was, she wasn't in any shape to take a call, especially from her dad. It wasn't just the lingering effects of alcohol; it was also the truth that she would spend more time on earth than her mom. That truth paralyzed her. That truth made her an emotional wreck. That truth drove her to do what she vowed she would make every effort to avoid.

She lied to Gunter. She lied because that was the only way she could protect him. "I had a wonderful time, Dad. It was a great birthday."

She lied because she had to. She had decided at an early age that it was her job to protect her dad from an unforgiving world. There were people, she discovered, who took great delight in witnessing misery. There were people who were skilled at knowing how to summon pain and suffering that resided deep within the soul of another human being. These people, she concluded, were followers of the devil. They performed the handiwork of an evil force. She needed to protect Gunter from such people, for the misery within his soul was not buried deep. As a child, she heard the pain that seeped beyond the confines of Gunter's office. She learned to identify the depth of despair by the tone and tenor of the sound. There were groans and howls, sighs and whimpers, each telling their own story. Each is connected to its own antagonist. Behind the sounds that Gunter's body pushed forth, inevitably the voice of Dolly Parton could be heard singing, "I Will Always Love You." Anya decided at an early age that she would not be counted among those who pierced Gunter's soul.

Therefore, she was hesitant to inquire about Katharina. She held her questions within her soul and waited for Gunter to grant permission to speak of her mom. Her body, too, would groan and howl, sigh and whimper as she lamented the absence of a mom, but such sounds never escaped her room. Her pillow became the sponge that absorbed the pain that spilled from her soul.

On the thirtieth day of May, two days after her twenty-eighth birthday, Anya acknowledged as she wished her dad a good week, that was not the first time she had lied to him. Looking at the pillow on the bed in her apartment in Chicago, she realized that she had been lying to him for years. She had been lying to herself as well.

Dusty's voice interrupted Anya's words. "No more. I can't lie anymore."

Gunter heard Anya's voice but could not discern what she had said, as he was listening to Dusty instruct Dillon to take the trail to the left that eventually would lead to the water.

Looking over his shoulder, Gunter asked, "What did you just say?"

"Uh, what?" Startled to realize that she had delivered that thought out loud, she stumbled to cover herself, "I must have been singing louder than I thought."

"Oh. What were you singing?"

"Umm, 'Fishin' in the Dark.'"

"Nitty Gritty Dirt Band?"

"Yeah."

"Hey, Bobby, 'Fishin' in the Dark.' You know it?"

"Oh yeah."

"Great! Tonight, campfire. You're playin' and Anya's singing."

"Sounds good to me. Let's hope, though, that by tonight we have some fish to show for our efforts in the daylight."

With a straight face, Dusty asked, "Hey, Dillon, don't you do ya jig to that tone?

With a smile that covered his entire face, Dillon answered back, "Boss, I don't know what you're talkin' about."

"I guess we just added one more to this evening's agenda. Campfire, Bobby playin', Anya singin', and Dillon dancin'." Gunter couldn't have sat any taller in the saddle as he spoke.

Under her breath, Anya cursed, "God, I have to stop lying. Look what I just got myself into."

With a simple wave, the three guys headed down the trail while Dillon, Gunter, and Anya attempted to negotiate the steep grade, better defined as a drop-off. The first fifty feet were straight down and ended with a switchback to the left, followed by several more switchbacks before reaching a clearing.

Reaching the first switchback safely, yet with her legs shaking, Anya said, "No downhill skier could have survived that drop, especially tucked in between all these trees. We made it down, but I can't imagine my horse making the climb back up."

Still smiling, practicing his dance moves in his thoughts, Dillon answered, "Oh, you'd be surprised what these horses can accomplish."

"I sure hope they can because there is no way I could make it up."

Taking the opportunity to have some fun at Anya's expense, Dillon added, "We could always put you on the mule. Mules are excellent climbers."

"Is he trained for riding?"

"No, but that's beside the point."

"Very funny. I can hardly control my laughter."

"He's telling the truth. Look at the mule's tail." Gunter joined in the conversation.

"I'm lookin', but I don't get it. All I see is a tail with some hair missing."

Gunter continued, "That missing hair, called a bell cut, tells you that this mule is trained for packing. A second shaved bell declares that the mule can pack and drive. A third means they pack, drive, and ride."

"That's pretty ingenious."

Dillon shared the origin of the bell cut. "It originated with the military. It was a quick way for personnel to determine what a mule could do, and it aided in the selection process."

"Why don't people cut a horse's tail to describe what it can do?"

"A horse's job, at least in the cavalry, was to transport people. Most horses were 'broke' for the purpose of riding and, if necessary, for driving. If a horse was broke to drive, they frequently were not broke to ride. The horse was viewed as a one-task beast. Mules were, first and foremost, pack animals, but they were also viewed as being able to drive and ride."

Gunter was impressed with Dillon's knowledge of military actions. "You did a bit of studying the history of mules and horses."

"Yeah, sort of. Last summer, the day after school ended, my father packed me up, hauled me out, and dropped me off at a camp in the wilderness of Utah. I had been hired to serve as one of the wranglers, which came as a surprise to me."

Anya asked, "You mean your dad planned this without your knowledge?"

"Yep. Our first task, literally, the day after I arrived, was to move a herd of a hundred horses more than three days out to a dude ranch. Oh yeah, I had never ridden a horse. I learned pretty fast how to stay in the middle of the saddle."

Attracted to the innocence of Dillon and the folly of the story, Anya continued to ask questions. "What were you thinking? What were the owners of the ranch thinking to send you out on that trip? Didn't they know you had never ridden?"

"I'm not exactly sure. And, honestly, I never asked. I needed the job. I'm sure they realized in the first three minutes that I had no clue what I was doing. Thank goodness for an old cowboy who took me under his wing. He was just like Dusty, only older."

"Older than Dusty?" Gunter was teasing Dillon, but he didn't catch on.

"Yeah, and what was really interesting was Old Buck wasn't in charge. He was just another wrangler. But he was ten times smarter than the guy in charge. Old Buck knew how horses think. As we rode side by side, he would frequently ask, 'Tell me, what's that horse thinking?' With a simple twitch of an ear or switch of a tail, he could tell me what the horse was thinking and what it would do next."

"I think Old Buck and my dad should get together. They would enjoy each other's company."

"Well, he'd have to travel to Utah because I don't think Old Buck is ever going to leave the state. To answer your question, Gunter, what I know about horses, I learned by the seat of my pants. The rest of the stuff I discovered after I got back home, and that came from reading."

"You were lucky, Dillon. You have had good teachers."

"My goal now is to start a mustang."

"Hey, Dad, isn't that on your bucket list as well?"

"What's that?"

"Starting a mustang. Isn't that on your bucket list?"

"It was at one time. Not sure I am up to the challenge anymore."

"I don't know, Gunter. From what I have seen, I think you would do just fine."

"That's kind of you, but honestly, these old bones just don't move like they used to."

The moment the threesome broke into a clearing, the conversation abruptly went from horses to fishing. Experiencing the sudden shift in focus served as a reminder, for Gunter and Anya, just how important the context can be to a conversation.

The horses and mule were secured, and with the fishing equipment in tow, the three pushed through a narrow band of thick brush and dense undergrowth that lined the stream. Emerging from the scrub, Dillon went to work tying a fly while Gunter and Anya stood like two petrified trees, admiring the scenery. Balancing atop two partially submerged rocks a few feet from the riverbank, Dillon started casting, as Anya asserted, "The movie, *The River Runs Through It*, could have been filmed right here. This is something to behold."

Dillon, while retrieving his line and flicking it back across the top of the water with the simple snap of his wrist, inquired, "Are you Brad Pitt or Craig Sheffer? Hey, isn't that your last name?"

"Not exactly, but it is close. Schaff."

"Oh, yeah, that's—hey!" Dillon's voice jumped two octaves, and it crackled. "I just had a strike. You guys better get your rods out, or I'm gonna clean out the stream. They are biting on dry flies."

The correct fly selection can make all the difference between catching fish and merely practicing one's casting. The conditions and the context dictate the proper fly to tie to the line. The lateness of the summer, the bright sun-filled sky, and the continual climb of the temperature suggested that dry flies might be the proper choice.

"What do you mean, dry fly? I suppose there are also wet flies?" Anya laughed as she asked the question.

Without looking at her Gunter said, "Well, actually, there are."

"Okay, Dad, just because we are fishing doesn't mean that I am going to bite, hook, line, and sinker on your little scheme to make me look foolish."

With his right hand held at shoulder height, Gunter said, "Honest, I swear, I am telling you the truth. There are dry and wet flies." Grinning, he added, "It pains me that you think I would do such a thing."

"Whatever, Dad. What's the difference, then? How do you know which ones to use?"

Dillon, while reeling in his first catch, said, "Ultimately, the fish tell you which fly to use."

"Boy, you guys don't give up, do ya?"

"The fish do tell you. If they don't bite after several casts, you change flies. You can change from dry to wet, or wet to dry. You can also change the color. The key is to select a fly that matches the type of bug that the fish are currently feeding upon. That's the context."

"That makes sense. What's with the dry and wet stuff?"

Dillon and Gunter cast a brief glance at each other as though they were determining if the response would be truthful or an attempt to make Anya look foolish.

With the hook removed from the trout's mouth and its tail frantically switched from side to side as it propelled itself away from Dillon's open hand, Dillon said, "You see my feet? I am standing out of the water. I am dry. That means I will be casting a dry fly. If I had waders on or didn't mind having wet feet and stood in the water, I would use a wet fly. In *The River Runs Through It*, they use a wet fly."

"So, we all will be using dry flies since we didn't bring waders with us."

"Yep, that's right."

With her finger pushing the flies around in the plastic container that Gunter brought to hold his collection of favorite flies, Anya asked, "Dad, which ones are the dry flies and which ones are wet?"

The moment Gunter and Dillon made eye contact, they started laughing. Dillon was so proud of his accomplishment that he momentarily forgot the precarious placement of his feet, which resulted in a loss of balance, and he started to tumble backward. His athleticism enabled him to right himself, but not before both feet landed in the water.

Anya desperately wanted to say, "serves you right," but instead, she calmly said, "I guess that means you now have to fish with a wet fly." Turning toward Gunter, she pretended to look disappointed when she inquired, "What's really the story with the dry and wet flies?"

"It refers to where and how the fish are feeding. If they are feeding on bugs underwater, it's wet, and feeding on bugs above water, it's dry. Wet flies sink into the water, and dry flies skim across the top of the water." Lifting a fly from the container, he said, "This is my favorite dry fly. It's called Parachute Adams, and the wet fly is Wooly Bugger."

Standing back on the rocks, with water having failed to penetrate his sealed boots, Dillon shared, "I'm currently using an Elk Hair Caddis, which is a dry fly, and it's workin' well." Before he completed the sentence, he was pulling in his second fish of the day. "Don't beat the water. Let the rod do the work."

Leaving his perch, Dillon moved in close to Anya, who was struggling to get her fly anywhere other than at her feet or two feet from shore but diving downward. "Relax a bit. It's not a tennis racket. The movement is more like the pendulum on a clock. It's smooth and consistent, and slow is not necessarily a bad thing."

Dillon continued to affirm her efforts, but very little was changing, and she certainly wasn't catching any fish, nor was she about to. Looking at Gunter, Dillon asked if he might make an observation.

With hesitation, he responded, "Yes, plus, any insight or assistance is greatly appreciated."

"That is a really nice rod and all. I mean, it must be fairly old."

"Both of these rods belonged to my grandfather."

"They are really nice, but—" Dillon stopped himself. It was clear he didn't want to offend Gunter.

"Don't worry. Share your thoughts."

"I think the rod is too heavy for you, Anya, as well as being too long. If you want, you certainly can try mine."

Letting her fly float in toward the shore, she asked, "What will you fish with?"

"I can fish any time. Here, take this rod and cast out."

"Oh, wow, it is light. Hey, look at that. I did it."

"Try to aim for that spot there in the middle and let the current push the fly downstream. If nothing bites, start again."

On her first cast to the middle of the stream, she hooked a fish. "I got one." Gunter, equally excited, instructed her to bring it in slowly.

Dillon added, "Depending on how they are biting, I try to set the hook and then give the fish more line for a few seconds before I start to work him in. But you're doing a good job. Keep it up."

"Boy, he's fighting."

"You're pulling him in upstream, so the current makes it more challenging," Gunter said. Bending down and reaching into the water, Dillon coached Anya. "Just a little more, and I can reach him. Nice. He's bigger than the two I caught."

Anya, feeling proud of her achievement, tried to downplay her excitement as she said, "Beginner's luck."

"Anya, you want a picture with that fish?" Gunter was already framing the picture.

"Yeah!"

Anya said "yeah," yet it came off sounding like the sun rises in the east and sets in the west. What could be more obvious? Of course, she wanted a picture.

Once the picture was snapped, Dillon explained how to release the fish. "You can just place the fish in the water and release the pressure, and you'll feel him sway to the right, then bend to the left, and he'll swim away."

A crease in Anya's brow accompanied her voice as she whispered, "Release?" Holding the fish tightly, she looked at Gunter, who nodded. A second time, she said, "Release?" Just as it was the first time, the word was drowned out by the sound of water surging around and over the rocks. She hadn't thought about what would happen once a fish was caught.

Release? It made sense, she supposed. Dillon had already done it twice, but as she watched him, it never occurred to her that she would be asked to do the same. Release? The word stirred within, and she realized there was something more to the act than simply a fish being returned to the water. Release?

She knelt and submerged the cutthroat in the water, and then, with the same precision as a surgeon with a scalpel, she slowly relaxed her fingers, and immediately the trout, feeling its freedom, swam away. Watching the fish make its way into the stream, Anya experienced a sense of peace she had not known for some time. Standing, she turned back toward Gunter, smiled, and nodded.

Dillon, unaware of what was transpiring between a father and his daughter, and a daughter and her father, asked Anya if she was ready to catch another.

"As long as it's not the same one, I'm ready."

Gunter set his rod aside and simply watched his daughter enjoy herself. He didn't need to catch a single fish to make this fishing trip a total success.

The next two hours were under the direction of Dillon, who led Anya and Gunter downstream in search of the next spot where the trout were waiting to feed upon the fly as it landed lightly atop the water. Each fish that Anya caught was documented on film. Even Gunter posed for a couple of pictures, as Dillon convinced him he needed to try his lightweight fly rod. At times, the trek downstream was more of an adventure than the actual task of reeling in a fish. Dillon, the mountain goat, also possessed the skills and balance of a funambulist, better known as a tightrope walker. Without looking down, he knew where to place his feet so as not to fall into the water. There was no path, no trail. A rope strung ten feet in the air would have offered more footing than available next to the water. In some places, the brush kissed the water, and in other places, the stone face of the mountain was the border that turned the stream. It didn't matter the terrain; Dillon was not to be kept from finding the next great fishing hole.

Having scaled an eight-foot rock formation and danced along the edge of the stream, like a ballerina on her toes, while clinging to the branches of the bushes, Anya and Gunter informed Dillon that they would eat lunch on a flat section of a rock while he continued to fish. With fish to be caught, Dillon wasn't interested in taking time to eat.

With a ham and cheese sandwich in one hand and a sketch pencil in another, Anya set to work sketching Dillon, with a fly rod in hand, against the backdrop of the mountains. Like Dillon, who never needed to look down, once Anya started, her eyes never left her model.

Gunter marveled at how she knew where her pencil was on the page. The pencil would stop when she took another bite of the sandwich and start again as she chewed.

"How do you know where you are on the page?" Gunter asked.

Continuing to sketch, she asked, "What's that?"

"How do you know where you are on the page without looking? How do you know you are making the lines where you want them?"

"Practice, I guess. You have to be quick because things change quickly. I don't want to miss the little things because that's what makes the sketch authentic."

"I don't know. I think I would be all over the page."

"It's like riding a horse. You don't have to look at the horse to know if it's moving correctly. You can feel it. Besides, I can always go back later and fix things that might be out of line or not quite right."

"I suppose you're right. I never thought of it that way."

"That's because riding is just a part of you, and sketching is something you view as outside of you, I dare say, any traditional artform. It's a mindset. But isn't riding a form of art?"

"Touché."

Before the sandwich disappeared, Dillon, with his fly rod fully in action, appeared in Anya's sketch pad.

Washing down the remains of his sandwich, Gunter inquired, "Want to talk about the struggle with releasing the fish? I can't imagine it was about the loss of eating the fish."

She laughed as she spoke. "Yeah, you're right. It was pretty small and wouldn't have been much of a meal. Plus, I know you would have made me clean it, and the thought of that—"

"What was it about, then?"

"I don't know. I suppose it had to do with our conversation last night and specifically the notion of letting Mom be who she is becoming."

"Are you ready to do that?"

"I'm getting close. There's one thing I need first. You've never told me about Mom's funeral."

"Her funeral?" Gunter turned his head from Anya and scanned the landscape on the other side of the stream. He searched, as far as the eye could see, to the right and then the left. Eventually, his focus landed back on his daughter. Even though she hadn't asked a specific question, he felt the need to explain. "It's not the sort of thing one just brings up in conversation."

"Why not? Was there something bad that happened?"

"Oh, good heavens, no. It was as beautiful and glorious as the scenery here."

Gunter's arm gestured across the air to include every aspect of the panoramic view before them. Before he realized it, he was describing Katharina's funeral.

"The days leading up to the funeral were a whirlwind of chaos. There are so many decisions that must be made in such a limited amount of time, that saying funeral preparations are stressful is an understatement. For example, selecting a casket. Your grandpa and grandma insisted on one specific casket. It was beyond the means of what I had available. If I remember correctly, it was called Solid Mahogany Hardwood Casket with Ivory Velvet Interior. Initially, I tried to convince them that your mom would never want such an item, but I came to realize that this was their way of trying to cope. Just so you know, if you place me in anything other than a pine box or the cheapest metal casket available, I promise you, I'm coming back to haunt you."

"I know, Dad. I've heard you say that before. Don't worry. I'll keep the cost of the casket to a minimum."

"The day of the funeral, the fifth of June, was a sunny day. It was a Saturday. You came home from the hospital on the first. Initially, the plan was for the funeral to be held on the fourth. But as word circulated of your mom's passing, I started to receive requests if the funeral could be on Saturday. Several of our friends from college wanted to attend the funeral, but they needed travel time. The day also made it easier for local folks to attend so they didn't have to take off from work."

"Was I there?"

"Oh, yeah. You spent most of the time sleeping, and when you weren't asleep, you were eating or pooping. Your grandmas were a huge help in taking care of you. Plus, there was no shortage of people who wanted to hold you. Kind of like a new puppy. Everyone wants to pet the puppy."

"Gee, thanks, Dad."

"What?"

"Comparing your only daughter to a dog?"

"I didn't say dog; I said puppy. They are always cute when they are little. If only—"

"Yeah, yeah." Anya playfully waved her hand at Gunter for him to continue.

"The service started in the rear of the sanctuary, where the pastor said a few opening words and invited everyone to stand and sing as the family followed the casket to the front of the church. We sang your mom's favorite song."

"Let me guess. 'Amazing Grace.'"

"How did you know?"

"We sang it at Grandma's funeral, and I figured there had to be something special about that song as Grandpa couldn't make himself sing a single note. Did anyone do special music?"

"There was. There was a high school girl who played her cello in church, and your mom loved how she played. The piece she selected to play was entitled 'Perfect.' And it was perfect. She played right after the sermon, and the notes brought to life every word of the message. The title of the sermon was 'A Flower Plucked From God's Creation.' I have a copy of the sermon. You can read it when we get home. From the church, we made our way out to the cemetery for the graveside service."

"I never told you, but god, I hated Memorial Day and going to place flowers on Mom's grave. I hated Memorial Day because it always landed close to my birthday, and it just made my birthday more difficult. I could go to the cemetery any other time, and it was okay, just not Memorial Day."

"I never knew." The sadness in Gunter's voice was discernable.

"How could you? I never told you."

146

"But I should have thought about the timing."

"Shoulda, coulda, doesn't get us anywhere." With a slight nod, Gunter thanked Anya.

"So, old man, do you want the same hymns sung at your funeral?"

"No. I want Marty Haugen songs."

"I love his songs. There are so many good ones. How does one select?"

"Already done, 'Gather Us In,' 'How Can I Keep From Singing,' and 'You Are Mine.' "I'm impressed, Dad."

"I don't want you to have to experience the whirlwind of chaos any more than necessary. A funeral can be a release, a letting go. Unfortunately, I just never let that happen."

"Letting Mom be who she is becoming." Anya's face was wet with tears.

"Yep," was all Gunter could manage to say as his cheeks also were growing moist.

Dillon, having just released another fish back into the stream, sensed that something unique was happening on the flat surface of the rock and, therefore, kept his distance as he spoke, "You don't have to fish anymore, but I just want to offer it up, since the afternoon is growing long."

Clearing his throat, Gunter answered, "Yeah, we want, we need to catch one more fish!"

Together, holding the trout Anya caught, Gunter and Anya knelt close to the surface of the stream, placed the fish in the water, and released it. Together they let the fish be who the fish was becoming.

Back at the horses, Gunter said, "When we get back, I have a song I want you to hear."

"When we get back home?"

"No, back to the tent."

She stopped her horse and turned toward Gunter, "You have music here?"

"I brought the MP3 player."

"Stop the presses. You brought the MP3 player? I didn't know you ever used that gift. My gosh, Dad. I am speechless."

A massive smile broke across Gunter's face. "Anya, there's a lot you have to learn about your old man, just as I have to learn about you."

Chapter 9

Having stroked his chin twice, Dusty spoke up. "I'm not trying to break up the gathering. I certainly don't want to infringe upon Dillon's dancing, and just so everyone knows, we can always toss more wood on the fire and keep it going as long as you all want. I merely want to remind everyone that breakfast is at seven tomorrow morning, and we have a fairly long ride tomorrow."

Standing in his usual spot outside the circle, Chuck asked Dusty to clarify the long ride in terms of hours.

"Well," again his hand washed over his face before he continued, "if we were to leave here by nine, we should arrive by three-thirty or four."

"In other words, between six and seven hours."

"Yeah, I would say that's about right. It depends on how long we stop for lunch. It's always nice to have a little time out of the saddle to stretch the legs and just get the blood flowin."

The bells were clanging by quarter to five as Quad and Brit brought the herd of horses and mules in from the far reaches of the canyon. The two wranglers must have headed out long before four since most of the herd had not been seen or heard from for more than twenty-four hours. The creek that supplied water to the camp zigzagged its way through the canyon. Hence, there was no reason for the stock to return to camp in search of water.

The clanging, combined with Dusty's words from the campfire the night before, had everyone up and dismantling their tents well in advance of breakfast. By the sixth day out, everyone knew the routine. Therefore, the teardown of the camp went quicker. The only difference was that after the group departed, the campsite would sit idle until next spring. There were additional tasks needing attention to "winterize" the site. Pipelines carrying water closer to the site needed to be drained so as not to burst when the temperature dipped below freezing. Canvases that served as cover for the feed and tack were folded and packed in amongst the gear. Logs cut to serve as stools were stacked in the kitchen area.

A few minutes before nine, the riders climbed onto the backs of their mounts, with Jack searching for a mound to aid in getting aboard his horse. The task of mounting a horse, which earlier in the week elevated the blood pressure for some, was performed without thought or stress. A horse that moved as a leg swung across its butt no longer yielded a squeal of excitement or consternation. The riders no longer formed a line before departure but simply waved to the wranglers, who finished tying the gear to the mules.

The only voice breaking the silence, of course, belonged to Chuck, who said, "We'll see you down the trail." Some things were not about to change after six days.

The first part of the morning trip was backtracking to the ranger's station. Even though it was the same trail ridden only a day and a half earlier, the ride was different. Viewing the scenery from a different vantage point can make all the difference in the world. Despite knowing that the bend in the trail was to the right or left, things previously hidden were revealed. Anya thought it was a perfect metaphor to accompany her dad's suggestion that they have a lot to learn about each other.

She entertained herself by pondering what it was she didn't know about him. Were there deep, dark secrets? She often acknowledged that she didn't know him, but she doubted that was what Gunter meant. She was pretty sure this knowing was different, more tangible if there was such a thing. Seeing the ranger's station in the distance, her thoughts shifted to herself. What had she hidden from him? What was it he wanted or needed to learn about her? Riding into the ranger's station for the first stop of the morning, she wasn't sure which was more threatening.

Before any of the riders could step down from the saddle, a woman stepped out of the tall grass and approached them. She appeared to be one of the Continental Divide hikers. The moment she uttered her first words, it was apparent that she hadn't spent her entire life in the States. In fact, after describing how she and her friend camped overnight on the riverbank, Chuck asked where she was from.

"Norway," she said with a smile. "My friend and I flew over the first of May and hope to reach Canada soon so we can get back in time for the start of the university."

As the conversation with the Norwegian continued, Anya was trying to determine her age. Eighteen, maybe nineteen. She wondered how this girl's parents allowed such a trip. She looked sideways at Gunter and wondered what he would have said if, at eighteen, she said, "I am going to hike across Europe for the summer. I'll be back in time for college." That got her thinking about what Gunter would not want to learn about his daughter.

The group wished the international hiker the best of luck and set off down the trail.

Anya continued down the path of considering what Gunter would prefer never to learn.

Would he want to hear how only two days after receiving her driver's license, she was pulled over by the police for speeding? She got off with a warning when the officer said, "Hey, you're Doc Schaff's daughter, right?"

Would he want to hear about the time she and her best friend snuck out of the house in the middle of the night to join a group of friends who went skinny dipping in the sand pit southeast of town? Or about the time in college, she singed her left eyebrow trying to drink her fourth Flaming Blue Jesus? Would he want to know that gunshots ring out in her neighborhood from time to time? That her car has been stolen twice and later found with only minor damage?

And more recently, would he want to learn that she fell in love with a married man? They had met through one of the popular dating sites. He was six years older than her, which he readily admitted when they spoke on the phone for the first time. On their first date, a meeting over drinks at the safe bar where she could easily escape with an authentic excuse, he explained that he had been divorced for little more than a year. He had two kids, a son in college and a daughter who was a junior in high school. He was a lawyer who was known for working crazy hours because, as he said, "I want to be a partner in the firm by the age of forty-five."

Their dates were sporadic for the first few months. She wouldn't hear from him for two or three weeks, and then he would call and say, "I'm free tonight. Let's go dancing." She was suspicious initially. It just seemed too perfect, too good to be true, but after being with him, it always seemed so right. She learned to accept the chaotic schedule of their relationship. She realized that she was falling in love with him. A year into their relationship, she asked when she would get to meet his kids. He became evasive, making excuses, and she again became suspicious.

One night, when out at a restaurant, he left his wallet at the table, thinking that she might pay the bill with his credit card. While he excused himself to use the restroom, she copied down his home address from his driver's license. He had been to her apartment numerous times, but she had never been invited to his home. She drove to the address in Forest Glen, knowing before she reached the address that this was the wealthy side of Chicago, and the odds were that a wife stood on the other side of the door. Would Gunter want to learn of her foolishness in dating a married man for more than a year?

Would he want to learn that he was going to become a grandpa?

Chuck's voice startled her. "Hey, to the right there, isn't that the trail we came up on?"

Jack, who was within earshot, said, "Yep, this is going to take us to Meadow Creek.

The terrain and scenery will change about ten times before we finally reach the campsite."

"Hey, Dusty, I could use a pitstop at some point." Alice just shook her head as she heard her husband's request. No doubt, in her mind, there was a more polite and civil way to announce he needed to pee.

Dusty turned around, while pointing forward, and asked, "That line of trees up ahead work?"

"They'll do just fine. Thank you, sir."

At the trees, Dusty announced that they would stop there for fifteen or twenty minutes. "If you want to snack, go ahead. We won't stop for lunch for roughly another hour and a half."

Shatz was great at packing an assortment of items in the lunch bag. In addition to a sandwich and cookie or a bar, there might be trail mix, mixed nuts, a granola bar, mini candy bars, and always fruit.

As the guys emerged from the trees, Chuck commented to Gunter and Jack, "The way you two drink coffee every morning, I can't believe how you can hold it until lunch."

Jack said, "What's to say we do?"

Chuck stumbled over a fallen branch as his head twisted toward Jack and fell headlong into Gunter's arms.

Assisting him back to his feet, Gunter added, "Why do you think we wear Depends?

Because they make us look sexy?"

"No, seriously. How do you do it?"

Jack, as stoic as possible, said, "We just told you. We don't."

Out of the corner of his eye, Gunter saw Chuck casually checking Jack and his pants for evidence of bulkiness that would suggest diapers. Jack and Gunter couldn't look at each other for fear of bursting out in laughter.

Grabbing his lunch bag from the saddle horn bag and taking a seat next to Anya, Gunter decided there were definite advantages to traveling with his daughter. Gunter's bag contained two small Twix candy bars, Anya's favorite, while Anya's bag had a mini Snickers and a mini Almond Joy, both Gunter's favorites. It didn't take any convincing on either's part to make an equitable switch.

Breaking apart the two-layered bars of Twix, having dropped the reins and letting her horse follow the tail of Gunter's horse, she knew he would want to learn about becoming a grandpa. One of the reasons for the trip was to surprise him with the news. Unfortunately, the right moment had not presented itself. The question that concerned her was, would he be supportive of the process she selected for making him a grandpa?

After ending the relationship with the married man and feeling sorry for herself, she used the situation to reflect on her life and what she wanted. She admitted to herself that she wasn't getting any younger. She had always wanted children, but she didn't want people asking if the child at her side was her grandchild. More than a year ago, she started exploring the option of adopting as a single parent.

Exploring the international options as a single woman, Anya discovered that India was one of the least restrictive countries governing adoption policies. Once she initiated the process, made her first down payment, and completed a preliminary evaluation, progress toward receiving a child moved more quickly than advertised. What was described as taking upwards of twenty-four months unfolded in just under nine months. The day before she left Chicago for the trip, she received a phone call informing her that a child was available for adoption. Upon her return, she would meet with a representative from the adoption agency to plan the first of two trips to India to complete the process. Savoring the final bit of chocolate, butterflies swirled in her stomach. The excitement made her giddy one moment and sweaty with fear the next. She knew for sure that she didn't want any discussion of a child to cloud any hope for a harmonious reunion with Gunter.

Having circled two massive mountain formations, at times riding at the base, at other moments halfway up, and still on other occasions more than three-quarters of the way up, the group started a slow descent toward a creek that teased them for the past hour with incredible, if not breathtaking sights. Within thirty minutes, they would be watering their horses in the creek and enjoying their lunch.

What appeared to be a question out of nowhere, as Gunter and Anya were perched on the trunk of a fallen tree, a moderate distance from the other riders, Anya asked, "We've heard Chuck reference his son and daughter frequently. Based on what you have seen of Alice and Chuck, are you surprised they have kids?"

"Honey," Gunter answered without removing his eyes from his sandwich, "after nearly forty years in my profession, I am no longer surprised by who has children."

"I know that, Dad, but that's not really what I am asking."

"Your question appears to be rooted in the assumption that Alice and Chuck planned to have kids."

"What?" Anya was startled by her dad's comment. "You don't think that's a safe assumption, based on what we have heard?"

"Again, after nearly forty—"

"Yeah, yeah. I get it." With a wave of her hand, she swatted the air between them. "Now answer my question."

"Does it surprise me?" Gunter shrugged his shoulders twice and wrinkled his face as he contemplated an answer. "No, not really. Does it surprise you?"

"It did at first. It really did. I don't know. For some reason I assumed as professional career people, they didn't have time for kids. I guess when they talked about all the international trips and places they have lived overseas, I—I don't know."

"But now you view them differently?"

"I don't think so. I just see how they fit kids into their lives."

"Ouch." Gunter turned and looked directly at Anya.

"I'm not suggesting they are not good parents. I mean, listening to Chuck, they have been active in their children's lives."

"But?" He leaned forward, anticipating the other shoe to drop. "Have they ever talked about how they met?"

"No, that's not a story Chuck has shared. He did talk about how when they were dating it was a long-distance relationship. He was in one country, and she was in another, both overseas. Does that somehow relate to their having kids?"

"No, it just occurred to me."

"Now, I am curious. Where did this question about children come from?"

"Nowhere. I was just sitting here and looking at them. She's reading while eating her sandwich, and he is working on a crossword puzzle, interrupting her for an answer every few minutes. It made me wonder what it is like in their home, and well, that led to the question of children."

"Got it." Gunter slid his bottom to the ground and proceeded to peel his orange as he deliberated on the notion of children. With a mist of orange juice squirting from his mouth, he spoke. "Children. It is an interesting topic to consider. Why do people have children?"

Without a moment of hesitation, Anya asked, "Why did you and Mom have me? Was I planned?"

"Oh yeah. You were planned. We had discussed having children and when to have children. We decided it wasn't fair to anyone, Mom, a baby, or me, to have that first child while I was immersed in medical school and Mom was working two jobs. Residency provided a much better time."

"Did you want more than one?"

Gunter leaned back against the trunk of the tree and weighed his response. "Your mom did. It wasn't an issue for me, the number or the gender. Well, that's not true. I wanted a girl."

"Why not a son?"

"I think I was afraid that I would pressure him to do the things I did or be better than I was. I guess I thought I would be more open to giving a daughter the space to be who she wanted to be."

"Speak for yourself, old man." Humor always drips with truth, and they both knew it.

The comment was safe to a point because it was funny, and yet the truth could be hidden.

Gunter nodded his head several times as though he was recalling instances when he may have pressured Anya to fit an image he desired. "Okay, I can admit, I always hoped you would find enjoyment in horses, but look where we are. They're not so bad, are they?"

"It's not just about horses. Overall, I think it was less about the obvious pressures, like horses, grades, that sort of stuff, and more about the silent, even hidden or controlled expectations you had. Maybe you didn't even realize you had these or were placing them on me. And not all of them were bad."

"You know, I think that's one of those 'sins of the father' that gets passed on from generation to generation. It's the struggle of being caught up in parenting without stepping back to understand what one is doing, why they are doing it, and how it is affecting their child. Which brings us full circle, back to the question, why children?"

"No doubt, there are many reasons."

"I agree. It might be for purely selfish reasons, for securing a place in the future, for an attempt to fulfill one's own unmet expectations or goals, but the one that scares me the most is that some people never answer for themselves, 'Why children?' They just do it!"

The topic Anya hoped might serve as a perfect segue into informing Gunter that he was going to be a grandpa diminished the longer the conversation evolved. The plan, developed within her mind and rehearsed numerous times, was for her to ask Gunter if he would be surprised if she were to have a child. But that didn't seem to be an appropriate question considering the twists and turns the discussion took since asking if he was surprised that Alice and Chuck had children. Taking a bite of her apple, she decided she'd have to wait for a better opportunity to tell him he was going to be a grandpa.

Departure from the creek was delayed until the pack animals crossed the creek and marched on past them. The tardiness of the wranglers was explained as the mules and horses stood and drank from the creek.

Quad described the first of two delays as he shared how they met the park ranger. "The ranger waved us down just before we hit the fork in the trail past the ranger's station and asked where we were headed. I told him Meadow Base Camp, and he said, 'It shouldn't be a problem, but be alert. With the heavy rain over the weekend, several grizzly sows with their cubs have been on the move. Again, shouldn't be a problem. Just giving you a heads-up.' We chatted for a few more minutes, you know, small talk, and then we pushed on."

Shatz moved her string of mules over toward Dusty, who stood on the shore and joined the conversation. "Did you tell him about the grizzlies?" she asked Quad.

"Yep," he answered.

"Did you tell him about the other reason we are late?"

"Was about to, but you pushed your way in."

"Well, I'll tell him. It was my fault after all."

"No, it wasn't. I watched it happen, and I didn't step in and stop it. That's part of my job as head wrangler."

Dusty stood patiently waiting for Quad and Shatz to resolve their mini dispute and share what happened.

"This morning," Shatz spoke softly, "when we were packing up the kitchen and, in particular, wrapping the stove, one of the guests asked if they could wrap the stove. I know that's our job, but I didn't want to say no."

"Is the stove okay?" Dusty inquired.

"It's fine. It just started sliding down on the mule. Dillon saw it right way and yelled, so it never hit the ground, but the mule was less than happy."

Dusty finished the sentence for her. "And he started kicking, which upset the mule behind him, and pretty soon, your string was all over

159

the place."

Shatz looked at her dad. "That's about the extent of it."

"I don't want to know which guest asked, although I'm sure I can guess. I trust the next time he asks, you will tell him no and why it's not safe for him to wrap." Dusty didn't wait for an answer from his daughter. He turned and walked toward the riders to tell them they would be leaving as soon as the pack train moved out.

The first half of the afternoon ride provided some of the most gorgeous views imaginable. The scenery grew in intensity as the trail wrapped around another mountain, descended into another valley, climbed another slope, and pressed on toward what resembled the outer petals of a flower opening. The views were aided by the fact that the area was lush with knee-high grass, the trees appeared to be planted strategically so as not to hinder but complement, and the rock formations added multiple colors and weight. A photographer or a painter could have spent a month in this seemingly untouched, unviolated corner of creation and not captured every aspect of its beauty, its grandeur.

Tucked in the crease of the petal of the flower was, in fact, a gorge. The full extent of the gorge came and went depending on where on the trail the riders were. The expectation among many of the riders was that passage through the narrow fold, created by a mountain on each side of a stream that bubbled with rapids, would occur as the trail dipped downward until it reached the water's edge and then worked upstream. Rounding the final bend of the mountain, forming one side of the gorge, proved that assumption was wrong. Passage through the gorge would not dip downward but soar upward.

Already more than halfway up the face of the mountain, the ascent began. Unlike the switchbacks on the first day of the trip, these were literally, at times, only separated by a foot or two. The horse and rider above could have reached out and shook the hand of the rider below. The grade of the mountainside dictated that each switchback only increased a foot or two upon the mountain. The width of the path narrowed to the point where a horse needed to remain in stride because the path was not wide enough for a horse to square up, in other words, to place both legs side by side. The sounds were few in number, but all were intense—the clatter of the horses' shoes on the rocks, the water hundreds of feet below pounding over the rocks, and a horse farting as it labored with each footfall to drive itself upward.

Not a single human voice was added to the sounds on the mountainside. It was as though giving voice to the moment might only function as a distraction. Some riders focused intently on assisting their horse in making the correct footfall. Others squeezed the reins more tightly as if that might help, and one kept their eyes closed, hoping the horse followed the lead of the one before them. The twenty-five-minute excursion ended as the gorge expanded in width, and the trail widened an inch or two and slowly began to drift downward. As the rocky path became more solid and the horses were expelling less methane, the riders relaxed, and their rhythm of breathing became more normal. Unfortunately, the scenery became less glorious as they traveled through long stretches of thick underbrush and eventually entered the forest. Nature's tunnel of trees stretched on for the better part of three-quarters of an hour until the tree line suddenly gave way to a massive meadow.

The descent into the meadow was steep, but the angle revealed that the wranglers were hard at work setting up camp. The site had the least number of accommodations upon arrival.

With no corral, a tie line had to be strung to which the horses and mules were attached. The kitchen area sloped considerably to the right as the only trees available to hold up the canvas cover were on the hillside. The stream that provided water for cooking or drinking was a quarter mile uphill. There was no pile of wood stacked and ready for heating the kitchen stove or fueling a campfire. The tasks were numerous, but with the assistance of everyone, the site took shape within an hour.

"I have to say, I'm glad this is our last campsite and not the first. I don't think we would have been much help the first few nights out." Chuck held the ax with both hands as he paused to catch his breath and share what was on his mind.

Dillon, who was feeding the log forward as Chuck hacked off another two-foot section, said, "We appreciate that you all are willing to jump in and help." He then added, "There's not much wood lying around here. Once we have this log cut, I'll grab the two-man saw, and if you're willing, we'll cut down a tree or two."

As the evening meal was concluding, Dusty turned to Quad, who was mopping up the last specks of food on his plate, his third helping, and said, "Once you're finished polishing that plate, you and Dillon can start turning the herd out."

"Sounds good, boss. Do you care who we leave behind?"

"The herd is probably going to stay mainly in the meadow tonight. Keep back my horse and yours. I have no idea what people may want to do tomorrow, but with these two, we can easily cut out two or three horses if needed."

"Okay, boss. Dillon, did you hear that?"

"Yep! I'll start at the far end. Have you decided who will carry the bells?" With a quick nod, Quad said, "Anyone that hasn't carried one this week."

As the boys ready the herd for release from the tie-line, Dusty alerted everyone to pay attention. More than likely, a horse or mule could pass by rather closely as they depart for the open spaces of the meadow.

On the previous nights, opening the corral gate was uneventful as the livestock quickly disappeared into the trees. Therefore, Dusty, along with the wranglers, didn't call attention to the event. This release had the potential to be different because there was a level of danger as the herd would, more than likely, pass close to the humans. They had little choice since they were tied next to the campsite. This release might be different because it had the prospect of being entertaining. The horses and the mules had not had an opportunity to roll at the conclusion of the trip. Once the saddle or pack was removed from their backs, they were tied to the line. Once free, some of the herd might drop and start rolling out the kinks, while others might bolt for the open spaces. Still, others might find the grazing near the campsite favorable. The entertainment existed in witnessing nature take its course.

The first fourth of the herd released kept their noses close to the ground and slowly pushed even with the campers. And then, having found the perfect spot, their front legs bent, their shoulders dropped, and the rest of their bodies slowly lowered to the ground. Without hesitation, their legs kicked out straight, and their butts gyrated first left, then right, then left again, as the animals rolled from side to side. The next group released, amounting to nearly half the herd, cautiously stepped around those on the ground before kicking up their heels.

Some in the herd leaped and spun, and cow kicked, as others raced at full speed for the center of the meadow, where, like the first group, they dropped and rolled. The final group lacked one defining act or action. They didn't move in unison. Instead, they resembled individuals doing their own thing. One rolled, another kicked, one darted across the meadow, and another trotted toward a pair that busied their mouths ripping up grass.

Gunter, like a kid in a candy store, stood mesmerized, attempting to absorb the entire scene. He paid attention to each horse and mule while noticing the entire herd. He noted which horse took the lead and which horses challenged that lead. Smaller groups of three or four animals formed, yet each subgroup moved in unison with all the other groups. After more than fifteen minutes of tag, rolling, kicking, and jumping, the entire herd settled down and grazed.

As that transpired, the two horses left behind were led from the tie-line to a makeshift fenced-in area where they, too, might enjoy the bounty of the meadow. Although the two didn't have the freedom to move as they might prefer, they remained a part of the herd as they called out and waited for a response.

Witnessing the herd expel enormous amounts of energy, despite the long day on the trail, invigorated the humans. What initially was perceived as being only a four- or five-log campfire expanded as the evening wore on, demanding the timber of a small tree. As one might expect, the conversation started with a recap of the day's travel, emphasizing the switchbacks. Several who experienced the flower petal gorge for the first time shared what they were thinking and feeling in the moment. The employment of all five senses was needed to capture and express the depth and breadth of the experience. The dusty, chalky taste of fear, the tingling of exhilaration, the simultaneous vision of grandeur and austerity, the pounding and the throbbing originating in the chest and pulsating in the ears, the pungent aroma of a body defecating at life's end.

Dusty summarized the gorge in one sentence: "I have yet to hear two people describe the experience in the same way." Which was the case for those seated at the campfire. The conversation that followed was not one but multiple conversations. Pockets of topics, like kernels of popcorn, swelled until they burst. People chatted with those next to them as well as across the fire. At times it was difficult to hear a response or a question as many individuals were speaking at once. That, however, ended abruptly when Brit, on the opposite side of the fire from Chuck, asked, "So, Chuck, I'm curious. How did you and Alice meet?"

Anya shot a look in Gunter's direction, shook her head, raised her shoulders, and turned her palms upward, informing him that she had nothing to do with the question.

Chuck, for the first time, was seated on a log next to the fire. When Jack set to work building the fire, Chuck arrived at the fire pit without Alice and proceeded to take a seat and assist Jack in the placement of logs and kindling. When others drifted over to the fire, including the arrival of Alice, Chuck remained seated. Everyone was aware of the change in his position at the campfire, but no one referenced the shift.

Chuck's chest expanded as he took a deep breath, and then slowly it returned as he exhaled. The pregnant pause continued. When he finally spoke, his answer consisted of three words. Everyone was in shock, including Alice, for he didn't elaborate on his answer. A chill raced through everyone's core as though they each participated in the Ice Bucket Challenge. It took several moments to recover.

"A blind date? Come on, Chuck. Gotta say more. You can't leave us hanging!" Jack's encouragement of Chuck was nearly as surprising as Chuck's three words.

Chuck twisted his head to the right and leaned forward slightly to look past Anya and into Alice's face. Anya, recognizing that she was in the middle of something, pulled back so Alice and Chuck could see eye to eye. Alice's expression never changed, nor did she say a word. Chuck sat straight up, with folded hands resting in his lap, and launched into the story.

"I was stationed in Korea. One of my overseas tours. Several of my buddies were on an assignment defined as accompanied tours, meaning their families, wives, and children, if they had children, accompanied them to South Korea. Each night they were able to return home to their spouse. Since this was the group of guys I spent time with, whenever we would stop for a drink, they would start pestering me about needing some female companionship."

Alice could only roll her eyes as Chuck spoke of sex in a non-direct manner. Everyone knew exactly what he meant. These were, after all, twenty-something-year-old guys. "I'd play along and say, 'How do you know I'm not looking or, for that matter, maybe I already have found someone. I just don't need to talk about it.' That usually just brought laughter as they would say, 'yeah, right.'"

Chuck took a drink of water before continuing. "One night, one of the guys, whom I would describe as my best friend, started to talk about going out on a blind date. He was saying how his wife knew this woman living in Seoul and teaching at the international school located on the base. Next thing I knew, there was a pile of money in the middle of the table, and I was being challenged."

"Our first date was a bet?" The edge in Alice's voice informed Chuck that it was in his best interest to carefully consider his answer before speaking. "How much money did it take for you to accept the challenge?"

For a brief interlude into the account of how Chuck and Alice met, everyone felt as if they were eavesdropping on a private conversation.

"First off, remember, this was a blind date. I didn't know who I was being set up with. And second, I would have paid you to go out with me once we met."

Alice spoke to the rest of the group. "Now he tells me."

Anya leaned in close to Chuck and whispered, "Nice touch."

Chuck responded, "I'm just being honest. The pile of money was about one hundred dollars. The money covered the cost of our meal, and I used the remaining money to buy the first round the next time the group went out. It was my way of saying thank you."

"Hey, wait a minute." Brit pulled back from the fire as she spoke. "I feel like we just missed a huge part of the story. We know the ending, but how did we get there?"

"As you now know, the date went well. We," Chuck looked at Alice as he spoke, seeking a nod of affirmation, "seemed to hit it off immediately. Our interests were, are, very similar. It was not difficult to maintain a conversation."

Alice offered the affirmation Chuck sought. She closed her eyes and nodded her head.

Without additional prodding, Chuck continued with the story. "Unfortunately, the timing of that first date was not ideal. It was the first week in May, and Alice was finishing up her last month of teaching at the school. By the second week in June, she was leaving for Morocco to teach at the Casablanca American School. Our budding relationship hit a potential roadblock. Quite honestly, my new best friend, the person whom I couldn't wait to see every day after Alice left Korea, was the mailman. Our relationship, Alice's and mine, continued to develop through snail mail. In hindsight, the physical separation was the best thing that could have happened. Our correspondence took us to levels we would not have reached if we were together." With an all-telling smirk, Chuck finished the narrative of their romance. "Needless to say, when we were able to be together, we cherished the time all the more and took advantage of every minute together."

Since it was Jack who pressed Chuck to elaborate on his three words, Quad thought it was only fair for Jack to share a bit of personal information. "Jack, what about your bride? I know you're married. I have heard you reference her. Anything you want to share?"

"If it wasn't for Martha, I wouldn't be sittin' here today." Jack pulled another swallow of Jack Daniels from his "drinkin'" tumbler. Jack carried two tumblers into the wilderness. One he described as his coffee mug, and the other was his drinkin' mug. They actually were tumblers complete with a cover to protect against any spillage of the highly valued liquids: coffee and whiskey. Jack wasn't shy about confessing, "I like my coffee, and I like my whiskey. I just don't like my coffee interfering with my whiskey."

"Lookin' at me now, it's probably hard to believe, but in my younger days, I was that young, unruly bronco that refused to be tamed. I was reckless. I rodeoed with dreams of making it to the big time. I would get on anything and try anything: bulls, bucking broncos, steer wrestling. I also enjoyed the lifestyle that went along with rodeoing back in the day. If you got hurt, none of us could afford to see a doctor; we just numbed the pain with alcohol."

"Is that still true today?" Chuck was always interested in learning all the details associated with any story.

Smoke drifted into Jack's face, forcing him to lean to the right as he looked across the fire to respond to Chuck's question. "Rodeo life today is a whole lot different than forty years ago.

My rodeo days ended with my body being pushed across the dirt by a ranked Brahman bull. I was loaded up and shipped off to the hospital. When I woke up, I was informed that I was lucky that I wasn't paralyzed from the neck down. The doc made it clear that with the condition of my spine, I might not be so lucky the next time. It was at that point that Martha walked into my life."

Bobby laughed and added, "Yep, and anytime he gets to thinkin' he is that young bronco, Martha takes ahold of the reins and reminds him he's been tamed."

"Does Martha have your same passion for horses and mules?" Anya asked.

"Nope, and that's what makes this whole thing work." Jack didn't waver as he delivered his response.

"How so?" Chuck, who just described the strength of his relationship with Alice based on the fact they enjoyed similar things, was curious to hear how Jack and Martha made it work.

"It's pretty simple. She does her thing, and I do mine. And it works." The nod of his head told everyone he was finished discussing the issue. He took another swig from his drinkin' mug and stared into the fire.

Dillon retrieved four logs to add to the fire, and the group watched in silence as the flames took control. The additional wood provided a ladder of sorts for the flames to climb and leap higher into the night air. Under the glow of dancing flames, Chuck turned to Quad and asked, "Forecast?"

The past few nights, Quad had become the prognosticator of the weather for the following day. It started quite by accident on Tuesday evening when someone asked if anyone knew the forecast for the remainder of the week. Quad raised his index finger, tilted his head back, scanned the sky, and said, "Sunny in the morning, intermittent clouds early afternoon, with partial sun by early evening." When Wednesday brought sunny skies in the morning, intermittent clouds in the forenoon, and partial sun in the evening, asking Quad the weather forecast for the following day became a part of the evening campfire. Although it had only been three days' worth of predictions, his batting average was over six hundred percent, certainly comparable to any meteorologist.

"Sunny in the morning, clouds building early afternoon, and partly cloudy by evening." Quad's forecast was accompanied by his index finger pointed toward the sky. Of course, Quad would never have identified the flexed finger directed toward the heavens as his index finger. He would have called it his trigger finger. Shatz, whose mind was on overload preparing for her exam, would have used the Latin terminology *digitus secundus manus*, better known as the second finger. Dillon would have demonstrated the correct word by pointing the finger in Quad's direction, and Dusty would have brought the whole discussion full circle by explaining how the word *index* is Latin, *indico*, meaning to point out.

Several people chuckled at Quad's forecast, as it became apparent that his predictions were basically the same every evening. His response to the interrogation was candid. "Once you have a good thing going, you don't give up on it. Until it fails you. If it rains tomorrow, tomorrow evening, you'll hear a new forecast for Sunday. As for now, I'm sticking with what I said."

Additional laughter erupted, confirming that Quad was in control of those who sat about the fire. It was clear he was enjoying the limelight, so much so that he picked up a conversation from earlier in the week that didn't receive much attention around the campfire, "Hey, Bobby, are there many cattle operations in Georgia?"

"Surprisingly, there are, and they are growing. The two main types of operations are cow-calf and purebred breeding. The most popular is cow-calf, and what most people don't know, and therefore what I think is interesting, is that most of the calves are shipped outstate."

"You'd be surprised," Quad picked up on the astonishment within the cattle industry, "how much movement of cattle there is. I don't mean shipping off to market, although that certainly is part of it, but as you said, movement of weanlings and bulls. Literally, across the entire country, cattle are being shipped. Early last spring, I was down in Texas on a ranch looking at a bull. I ended up purchasing the animal and hauling him back to Big Timber. Our ranch is south of I-90."

"I'm not sure I understand. Why would you need a bull from Texas? Is there something special about this particular bull?" Anya's question matched the puzzled look on her face.

"He is special, alright. He fits our breeding program, which is pure-bred breeding, and he has a track record of throwing males."

"And that's important, because?"

"The success of our program is that we have bulls that can be bred to a variety of breeds and produce effective stock. The bulls pass on qualities to their offspring that other ranchers and cattlemen desire. There is a market for that type of bull. So, each spring we hold an auction in Miles City where we sell the bulls. It's just nuts, all the work that goes into the one day, but that event floats the business for another year."

"And all the bulls sell?" Chuck slid to the edge of his log as he was being pulled further into the details of the auction.

"Just about all of them. Sometimes, a person will lease one of the bulls, meaning they pay us for the use of the bull, and then once they have the cows bred, they return the bull. It's a great deal."

"I wonder why my wife hasn't thought of that."

Everyone froze, including Quad, who was at a total loss for words. The fire dimmed momentarily as everyone inhaled at the exact same moment, drawing oxygen away from the flames. Slowly, Chuck's eyes moved around the circle. He expected to hear laughter and see smiles. Instead, he was greeted with blank stares. Until his eyes drew even with Alice.

Fiery flames darted from her eyes. It was difficult to determine if she was angry or more hurt, perhaps even humiliated by her husband's attempt at humor at her expense. Of course, Chuck never meant it as an embarrassment to Alice. He was simply trying to be one of the guys discussing sex. What he failed to grasp was that such locker room humor was belittling to every female, as well as male.

What started as a tender moment for Chuck and Alice, as he described the early stages of their relationship, ended with pain and disappointment. Alice never spoke another word following Chuck's faux pas. However, as her body slowly disappeared into the log and the blood drained from her face, leaving behind a ghostly figure, the words, "How could you?" didn't need to be delivered into the night air. Witnessing the transformation of his wife, Chuck realized the consequences of his macho adolescent behavior and the depth to which he disappointed Alice. His body was also transformed. Unfortunately for Chuck, as he shrunk into the log, he couldn't vanish from sight, no matter how much he wished he was invisible.

For the longest time, no one spoke. The additional logs Dillon had added to the fire were nearly nonexistent. The words that finally broke the tension were accompanied by a voice that cracked and wavered slightly. "I am sorry. That was a stupid thing to say."

Chuck then stood and excused himself from the circle, and Alice followed him to their tent. Others slowly bid one another goodnight and departed for their tents.

The fire, a mere remnant of the light and heat it provided earlier in the evening, reflected the mood that gripped the meadow. Beneath the distant clang of a bell or two, Dusty spoke to the wranglers in hushed tones. He invited them to share what they were feeling and thinking as a way to discuss what happened. Each of them knew, and each had experienced the fact that people journey into the wilderness for a host of reasons. Each of them had experienced tension, even conflict, among guests. The key is to monitor each situation, giving people the space needed to meet their objective for the trip or to solve an issue. The key is to know when to be silent and when to step in so things don't get out of hand. Dusty trusted each of the wranglers, but there also wasn't anything wrong with a simple reminder.

"There are two more full days remaining. Let's do everything possible to make them as good as the first six."

Nearly in perfect unison, Quad and Dillon said, "Sounds good, boss." Into the darkness of the night, the campfire was left to die.

In the tent, tucked comfortably in her sleeping bag, Anya asked, "Where's the MP3 player?"

"Here, in my duffle bag, probably near the bottom." Gunter pulled the bag closer to his sleeping bag and started pulling out articles of clothing to reach the bottom.

"When did you start adding music to the device?"

"I don't know. A while back, I guess."

"You do know that your phone has the same capabilities as the player, right?"

Shaking his head, he said, "You and that phone."

Ignoring that comment, she asked, "What's this song you want me to hear?"

"It's a very simple title, 'Fall on Me.' It is a song sung by the father and son duo Andrea and Matteo Bocelli. Matteo sings in English and his father in Italian."

"I've not heard of it."

"Before you listen to it, let me explain. The very first time I heard the song, I thought it was about Katharina and me. You will hear the words, '*I close my eyes, and I see you everywhere.*' I do see your mother everywhere. But it's not about Katharina and me. You know the song that belongs to your mom and me, 'I Will Always Love You.' Ironically, a month after I first heard the song, I saw an interview with Matteo where he described the song as a song about fathers and sons. At that moment, I realized why I enjoyed the song. It is also a song about fathers and daughters. Anya, this is our song. As the refrain says, '*Fall on me, with open arms ...*'"

Gunter was about to continue speaking the words but stopped, switched off his light, and pushed play. Two pianos performed the interlude, and then one voice sang, followed by another, and before the piece ended, the voices sang together, *"Fall on me."*

Silently, Anya wept. Emotion, passion, and love flowed from her body as she listened to each word. For this, this is what she had always wanted. Simply and quietly, to fall on her father.

Chapter 10

The coffee club, Jack, Bobby, and Gunter assembled in the make-shift kitchen, where Shatz was busy making breakfast. With each of the mugs filled to the brim, the three parked their bottoms on the three-legged collapsible stools Dusty packed.

"The tent is still standing," Jack said as he looked out into the meadow.

"You sound like you're surprised. Were you expecting it not to be?" Gunter didn't need to follow Jack's line of vision to know that he was referring to Chuck and Alice's tent.

Before Jack could respond, Bobby joined the conversation. "I don't see a sleeping bag outside either."

"Based on what we saw last night and then the mumbled voices we heard after we crawled into our tent, yeah, I'm a bit surprised. I wasn't sure what to expect once the sun rose." Jack looked directly at the morning sun as he spoke.

"If you heard them talking last night, that's a good thing. Alice wasn't speaking when she left the fire." Gunter took a small sip of his coffee, which had cooled down two degrees below boiling.

"She was speaking alright, that much we know for sure. We couldn't hear specifically what was said." Bobby smiled as he finished his comment. "But speaking from experience, I'm not sure it was necessarily a good thing."

Jack and Gunter chuckled and nodded their heads as though understanding exactly what Bobby meant.

Even though he partially agreed, Gunter offered a rebuttal. "That's probably true, but at some point, they have to discuss it. She needs to be able to express her anger or frustration, or whatever she felt. They can't pretend it never happened."

Wiping a bead of coffee from the rim of his coffee mug that threatened to drop, Jack added while inspecting his mug for a leak, "Yeah, and based on what we have heard from Chuck this week, I doubt this is the first stupid thing he has said. He sorta talks and then thinks about what he said."

Bobby looked in the direction of Chuck and Alice's tent as he said, "I know one thing for sure; if I had said that and my wife was sittin' at the fire, I wouldn't have been sleepin' in the tent. And I wouldn't blame her one bit for kickin' my ass out of the tent."

Jack looked at Bobby and said, "You'd be lucky if that was all she did to your ass." "Forgiveness is an amazing thing."

Jack couldn't believe what he just heard Gunter say. "You think she'll forgive him that quickly?"

"Yeah," Gunter said as he nodded several times. "Based on what I have heard Alice say throughout the week, I think she will. Besides, a marriage can't survive without it. For that matter, humanity can't survive without it."

Turning his attention back to the kitchen, Bobby asked, "So why doesn't it happen more often?"

"I don't know." Gunter grabbed the brim of his tattered Stetson and lifted it slightly, exposing more of his forehead. It provided a moment to ponder what to say next. "Maybe it's too risky. Forgiveness requires that the one doing the forgiving becomes vulnerable. That opens one up to being hurt again. And, of course, there's that overused saying, 'Hurt me once, shame on you; Hurt me twice, shame on me.' But Jesus said, 'I don't say forgive, seven times seven, but seventy times seven.' Meaning, there are no limits to forgiveness."

"Yeah, but doesn't that cheapen the whole thing?" Bobby asked.

Gunter turned to Jack and asked, "Jack, does your wife say, 'I love you?'"

Without a moment's hesitation, Jake said, "Sure."

Gunter continued, "Can she say it too much that it becomes cheap?"

Jack leaned forward and said, "I understand what you're sayin', but that's not what I'm talkin' about. I was thinking about what if we forgive someone and they aren't sorry?"

Without saying a word, Bobby nodded his head in agreement.

Gunter paused for a second and then said, "What you're suggesting is that forgiveness is dependent upon hearing an apology."

Jack placed his hands on knees leaned against the back of his chair and nodded as he answered. "Yes, exactly."

Looking directly at Jack, Gunter returned to the topic of love to make a point. "Has your wife ever said, 'I love you,' and you were not worthy of her love?"

With a partial chuckle, Jack said, "Hell yes."

"So, why is it any different for forgiveness? Perhaps in the act of forgiveness, one becomes remorseful, one apologizes, one acknowledges that they were wrong, causes harm, fell short of expectations."

Leaning back ever so slightly, so as not to tip backward, Bobby said, "I never thought of it in those terms, but that makes sense. You think that is what Alice is doing?"

"I don't know. I really don't know." With his coffee several degrees cooler, Gunter swallowed a mouthful and finished his thought. "But what I do know, what I have experienced is that the most challenging forgiveness isn't always that which is directed toward another, but the act of forgiving oneself."

With that, Gunter stood and said, "I better go and make sure Anya is awake. She was pretty tired last night." Gunter smiled as he walked toward the tent, thinking about the process of forgiving himself. He hoped Chuck could do the same.

Kneeling in the opening of the tent, with his knees on the tent floor and his boots on the grass of the meadow, Gunter patiently waited for the cool morning air to circulate through the tent. Rather than use his voice to rouse Anya, he decided to use nature to accomplish that task.

He didn't need to wait long before Anya offered up a comment. "Yes, Dad. I'm awake. You can close the tent flap."

"Yes, I could, but I also know you well enough to know that if I don't see your face, you will drift off back to sleep before the zipper reaches the bottom of the flap."

She turned in her sleeping bag and tilted her head forward. "Satisfied? I'm awake."

"Thank you. Breakfast should be ready in about fifteen minutes."

"You know, Dad, you look like a grizzly kneeling there in the entrance to the tent."

"*Grrrr.*"

"Yeah, well, that's a pretty sick grizzly."

"Sick or just old?"

"Probably both. But that beard is looking really unkempt. I can't remember you ever having a beard."

"Part of the profession."

"What, doctors can't have beards? What, people don't trust doctors with facial hair? Is there some unwritten social norm?"

"That's possible, but that has nothing to do with me not growing a beard."

"I'm glad. I would have been very disappointed. I have never known you to cave to social pressure."

"It's the issue of cleanliness. I never wanted to wear a netting over the beard. Too scratchy. Yet, you can't risk having a hair drop onto a patient during surgery."

"I think it's funny that you, Jack, and Bobby didn't shave the entire week, but Chuck shaved every day."

"Funny, how so?"

"I would have guessed if anyone wasn't going to shave, it would be Chuck as a way of bonding."

"Bonding over a beard?"

"Yeah, you know, one of the guys. That was the whole point of his comment last night, right?"

Gunter, at that moment, decided not to go down that road again. Instead, the topic of a beard felt less taxing. "You're questioning why he didn't grow a beard?"

"I suppose I am, but it sounds silly when you just asked the question."

"Maybe it's uncomfortable. You know, irritates his skin." With a shrug of his shoulders, he added, "Or maybe Alice doesn't approve of beards."

"If I had to guess, based on those options, I'd say Alice is the cause."

Leaning back so his head was now outside the tent, Gunter felt a twinge of sadness as he looked across the meadow to Chuck and Alice's tent out of the corner of his eye. It might well have been Alice that forbade Chuck from growing facial hair. But that wasn't what poked at Gunter's insides. Rather, it was the isolation he assumed Chuck had experienced most of his life. It's one thing to be lonely and quite another to be isolated in the midst of others. It's one thing to separate oneself from others and quite another to be dismissed, reviled, and scorned by one's own values. The frustrating truth was that the harder Chuck tried to be visible, the easier it was to ostracize him.

Anya finished her thought, "But you know, it's really none of our business."

Gunter stuck his head back inside the tent and said, "I agree!"

"Agree or not, you still look like a grizzly. Go back and get more coffee, and I'll be there in time for breakfast."

Anya didn't need to rush. As it turned out, other than Jack, Bobby, Gunter, Dusty, and Shatz, who stood by the stove ready to serve, the remainder of the crew took their time in arriving for breakfast. It truly was a lazy Saturday morning. Even after the food was gone and the dishes were washed and returned to their proper box, no one left. The farthest anyone went was to the campfire pit, where logs provided a backrest as one gazed out into the meadow and the massive mountain ridge across the way.

It reminded Gunter of when he was a kid, and together with his parents, they would spend Christmas Eve at his grandpa and grandma's house. What made it even more exciting was the fact that it wasn't just their family who spent the night, but two of his mom's sisters and their families also spent the night. The other three sisters and their families would return on Christmas Day for the noon meal. Since all the gifts were opened on Christmas Eve, and no one went to bed before three in the morning, Christmas morning was a slow, relaxing time. Other than Grandpa, who rose early, along with Gunter, to milk the cows, everyone else slept in. When the adults did start to rise, movement was pretty slow. Some shuffled their feet because they drank too much the night before, while others stepped cautiously because the floor was tough on their bodies. Yet, each Christmas morning was highly anticipated because they all wanted to be there.

And so it was in the meadow at the base of the Continental Divide. The entire group wanted to experience the beauty, the splendor, and the solitude together. Silence from the night before, rooted in uncomfortableness, was transformed into peace and serenity. The vast wilderness of the Bob transformed a handful of strangers into companions. It makes sense that cowboys, back in the day, referred to their colleagues as partners. No one from the group ever said, "Howdy partner," but it would have fit.

Without any prompting from Dusty, Gunter and Anya expressed that their desire for the day was to ride the ridge across the meadow, the Continental Divide. The request ended with a question, "Is it possible, first, to reach the ridge on horseback and second, to ride along the Divide?"

Brit, as though she just discovered that her backside was sitting on a nest of fire ants, leaped into the air and said, "If it's possible, I would like to go with them."

Dusty, as expected, considered the request for a minute or two before he spoke. "You'll have to cut your own trail to reach the top of the ridge, but yeah, once you're there, for the most part, it's pretty wide. Not a problem for the horses." Gesturing toward one part of the mountain where a peak sprang up, Dusty said, "I probably would leave the horses at the base of the peak there and climb it myself. Not that they couldn't climb it, but the very top can't hold more than three people on foot. It would get terribly crowded up there, and you want to stop and enjoy the view. Okay, Brit, you go with Gunter and Anya."

Alice, whose voice hadn't been heard much during breakfast,

shared that she and Chuck would like to hike to the Continental Divide. To which she quickly added, "At least, that's our goal. Whether we get there or not, doesn't really matter."

Quad offered to accompany them. "As many times as I have been back here, I have yet to hike that ridge."

Dusty turned to Jack and Bobby, "You guys up for a horse ride?" Both nodded without any hesitation.

"There's an old hiker's cabin back on the other side of the mountain from which we came. The ride isn't easy, but there's a lotta history up there, and the view is spectacular."

"Boss, you want us to stay in camp? Otherwise, Shatz and I were thinking about hiking that mountain to the south there and trying to come around the backside."

"Yeah, it's possible. I did it as a kid. Probably not much of a trail anymore, besides elk and goat trails."

No one said it, but there was a moment of disappointment that spread amongst the group of partners when Dusty didn't share the story that accompanied his exploration of the mountain trail. Everyone, including Shatz, respected Dusty and the folk wisdom he weaved into every story. Therefore, they felt slighted when he didn't explain why, as a kid, he hiked that mountain.

Following his own moment of reflective silence, Dusty concluded, "Yeah, I think everything should be okay here. The herd, other than the six horses we use, are all out in the meadow. We can cover everything up. Sure, go ahead."

Dusty offered one final comment to the wranglers before everyone departed to prepare for the day's adventure. "I don't expect any problems, but as always, make sure you have the bear spray."

In unison, clearly, they had practiced, the four wranglers said, "Yes, boss."

Horses saddled, with lunch in their saddle horn bags, Gunter, Anya, and Brit headed east out of camp, as Jack, Bobby, and Dusty headed back to the west from which they came the prior afternoon. Alice, Chuck, and Quad had departed thirty minutes earlier, realizing that if they were to make it to the top of the ridge, they needed to leave sooner rather than later. Dillon and Shatz, not concerned about the time factor but driven by the thrill of cutting their own trail, left just minutes after Alice and Chuck.

The march across the meadow was less than pleasant. From a distance, the meadow looked like a paradise, lush with small summer flowers budding forth and endless green patches of grass. Once in the meadow, a different story emerged. It was lush with greenery, but such was the case because much of the meadow was lush with water. The area was as much an endless bog as a meadow. The horses sunk deep into the muck, and the sound of suction followed nearly every step. The three tried to find dry ground, which lengthened the trip across the meadow. They weaved first to the left, then to the right, straight for a short distance, then right, left, right, back left, and straight. It was only once they reached the trees that the ground became firm.

The rising of the mountain from the meadow provided the first of several obstacles. The base of the trees was snarled and entangled with thick undergrowth, making it challenging for the horses to push through. Where the undergrowth was minimal, or at best manageable, the limbs from the trees hung low, so each rider spent most of the time hugging their horse's neck. The elk and goat trails meandered far and wide, so their value often was short-lived. It didn't take long before the three dismounted and led their horses on foot. The ascent was slow, and climbing on the western face of the mountain increased the temperature with the sun beating down upon them.

The edge of the tree line enabled the three to mount their horses and continue toward the ridge. There was no time restraint on the day's adventure other than nightfall, yet there was an element of angst. They had already spent more than an hour and a half crossing the meadow and making their way through the trees. If Quad's weather report was correct, clouds would roll in early afternoon. With the promise of spectacular views awaiting them, no one wanted to jeopardize the prospect of being awe-struck by the possible arrival of low-hanging clouds. With no visible trail leading to the top, Gunter pressed his heels against the horse's belly, prodding him to take the lead. He knew that the gelding was comfortable being out in front.

Some horses make great trail horses, provided they are in the middle of the chain. Place these horses on either end, and they begin to unravel. Any small sound results in increased anxiety and the potential for unexpected behaviors. Sudden stopping, repeated attempts to turn around, to retreat, kicking out. The list goes on.

Gunter and the gelding understood one another by this point in the trip that it didn't take much for his horse to lengthen his stride and pull ahead of the other two horses, who formed a line behind. The first several hundred yards were difficult for both horse and rider as the footing was unpredictable. This was the area where the rocks that tumbled from high above came to rest. Beneath the weight of the horse, the rocks were in constant movement, slipping downward, sliding to the right or the left, which inevitably brought more rocks down from above. A mini avalanche of rocks developed. Horse and rider needed to stay atop the ground that was shifting beneath them. Gunter realized that the best way to navigate the climb was to create their own path of switchbacks. He stopped briefly to inform Anya and Brit of his plan.

"I think our best course of action is to start switchbacks. Pull in behind each other, but leave some space in case the horse ahead of you starts to slide downward." And then, almost as an afterthought, he added, "I don't think we will backtrack and come down this way. Hopefully, once we reach the northern end of the Divide, we will find a place less rocky. From camp, it looked like there might be a drainage ravine we could use to come down. Either way, we first need to get to the top."

Both Anya and Brit agreed with Gunter's plan, trusting that he knew what he was doing while trusting their horses even more, which is precisely what Gunter was doing as well.

The time on the cell phone, the modern-day pocket watch, displayed 1:12. Even without cellular service, Brit's phone functioned as a camera and an alarm. With horses and riders exhausted, the three decided to stop and relax with a sandwich before starting the ride on the Divide.

Refreshed and excited to begin their ride on top of the world, or at least on top of a ridge that determined the flow of water, they packed up and moved out. Less than a quarter of a mile into the ride, Brit's horse came up lame.

"Hey, guys, we need to stop and check my horse. He seems to be lame on his right front leg."

An examination revealed that he threw a shoe, probably back in the meadow. The suction from the muck, no doubt, pulled it off. The result, whatever was responsible for the missing shoe, was that a chunk of his hoof wall was torn out. Gunter suggested that, more than likely, the limp was the result of bruising the sole of his hoof on the rocks below because there was no shoe to protect that area. That conclusion made sense until Gunter noticed a cut.

Lifting the gelding's right front leg to examine the entirety of the hoof, Gunter was immediately greeted by a sizable cut on the coronary band, the portion just above the hoof. The cut was located on the back side of the leg and was noticeable only as the leg was lifted. Gunter knew the seriousness of the injury and the potential that if not treated correctly, it could result in permanent damage to the horse.

Carefully returning the hoof to the ground, he said, "He's not ridable, Brit."

She understood the severity of the cut. "You think we can lead him back down?"

"I'm no vet, but if we wrap it tight and don't add any additional weight, I think that's our best option, probably our only option."

Anya spoke up. "I still have that vet wrap you gave me a couple of days ago in the saddle bag."

"Good, grab it. We'll wrap it to help keep the swelling down for now."

Stroking the horse's mane to reassure him that he was in good hands, the moment Gunter finished, Brit said, "You two continue, and then come back, and we'll walk this guy down the mountain."

Anya, holding the lead ropes to her horse and Gunter's, said, "No, that's okay. We can head back now."

"Hey, I know you both have been looking forward to riding the Divide. Now get. The longer we stand here and argue, the later it will be when we get back. Now scoot!"

Anya and Gunter looked at each other, knowing Brit was right. It was Anya who vocalized their consent.

"Yeah, you're right."

"I know I'm right. I'm always right."

The three of them laughed, and Anya said, "No, that privilege is reserved for my dad."

As the two of them started to ride to the north, Brit yelled and waved frantically. "Wait, wait. You need to take the bear spray."

Armed with the bear spray tucked in Anya's saddle horn bag, they trotted off, one on each side of what they considered to be the Continental Divide.

Lifting the reins slightly, both Gunter and Anya slowed their horses down to a walk. The path narrowed in spots, making it difficult, even dangerous, to attempt to ride side by side. Beneath a faint breeze blowing across their faces from the northeast, they were silent as the scenery washed over them. To their left, they could see the tents on the far edge of the meadow. The gorge they passed through the previous day was behind them and was followed by another mountain peak and another mountain still even higher. To their right was a lush valley even greater in size than the meadow. The contrast of mountain and valley appeared to press on indefinitely. At that moment, they were riding on top of the world.

Stopping his horse and with both hands resting atop the saddle horn, Gunter turned toward Anya and asked, "Do you think we should be riding on the same side? I feel as though the divide that separated us has narrowed, if not disappeared."

"Nah, I think it's good that we ride on each side. This is who we are. We provide balance for each other. You might even say, we are sort of yin and yang on top of the world as well as in daily life."

"Yin and yang, huh? Am I yin or yang?"

"See, there it is. I would never have thought to ask that question. I would have simply cherished the thought of the wholeness that we create together. We add depth to each other's life. We complement the other."

"Yes, we do."

As the horses started to walk forward, Gunter again asked, "Seriously, am I yin or yang?"

"Does it matter?"

"I'm not totally sure, but it feels like it should."

"Well, let me think for a moment." The horses took several strides before Anya spoke. "If I remember correctly—it has been a while since I studied this in college—the Chinese story is that yin and yang were born in chaos and existed in the core of the earth."

"Born in chaos. That's sounds a bit familiar."

"I suppose, but I didn't know any different. Anyway, back to yin and yang, at the center of the earth, they established harmony and balance, and from this, the first human was created. Although each is assigned either feminine or masculine attributes, they aren't themselves female or male. They are meant to represent opposites that together and in unison form harmony and balance."

"So, what you are suggesting is that it doesn't matter if I am yin or yang, but that I am one and you are the other, and together, in unison, in the midst of the chaos that surrounds us, we create harmony and balance."

"Yeah, that's what I'm saying." Anya smiled without taking her eyes off the makeshift trail that seemed to be narrowing.

Nodding his head, Gunter said, "Yeah, I'd have to agree."

Cutting him off, Anya asked, "Hey, Dad, how's your horse?" The pitch in her voice was an octave higher.

Recognizing that fear captured Anya, Gunter responded as calmly as possible, "Fine, why?"

"It may be nothing, but my horse seems nervous. He keeps slowing down as though he doesn't want to go any farther. I have to kick him to keep up with you. You don't think—"

Gunter cut her off before she could get the words out. "He looks okay. Maybe he's still waiting for Brit's horse to catch up."

"Yeah, that's probably it."

"Wow, look at that view. And to think that we are riding on the very space that determines which way the water flows." Digging in his saddle bag to locate his camera, he asked, "How many pictures do you have left?"

"I think I have six left. Two more for today and then four for tomorrow."

"I have eight. I'll take the next couple, and you save yours for later."

Dropping the reins to steady the camera with both hands as the gelding walked on, Gunter snapped three photos. Tucking the camera back into the saddle bag, Anya informed him that she had something important to share with him.

"I have something to share with you that I think will top any view from here."

"I'm all ears."

"Dad, you are going to be—DAD!" Anya screamed as her horse swung around and started dancing. On the narrow rim of the ridge, her horse hopped, first to the right and then left. She fought to keep her eyes open so as not to become disoriented. If she had not held the reins taunt, pulling the hackamore against the bridge of the horse's nose, he would have raced off at full speed. Instead, the gelding did the only other thing he could; he continued to turn in circles.

It was amazing that Anya had been able to hang on. Gunter taught her well. If you start to lose your balance, squeeze your thighs and grab the saddle horn. That action will keep a rider in the center of the saddle. In addition, if possible, keep your heels down. That simple act will make it easier to keep your feet in the stirrups and avoid kicking the horse's sides, which will only increase his speed.

Over the snorting and huffing sounds coming from her horse, who stopped spinning in an effort to paw at the rocky surface, Anya shouted, "Dad, what's that noise?" With the horse's shoulders bobbing up and down, sparks flared as the metal shoes struck the rocky surface. Anya screamed as loud as possible, "DAD, BEHIND YOU!"

When Anya's horse started to dance, Gunter turned his horse toward Anya in hopes that, together with Monte, they could bring some calming presence to her horse. In response to his daughter's directive, he draped the reins across Monte's neck, spun the horse to the left, and came face to face with brown fur.

"GRIZZLY! Go, Anya. Go."

Monte instinctively reared and kicked out his front legs as a defensive response. Gunter stayed put despite the repeated attempts by his horse to push the grizzly back. Each rearing up only brought the grizzly closer. With its mouth wide open, baring its teeth and growling, the grizzly reared up and swung outwardly with her powerful front leg. The swing was more powerful than any Sammy Sosa or Mark McGwire swing of a baseball bat.

Attached to her swinging club were razor-sharp two-inch nails that could rip the siding off a house. To avoid being struck and slashed open by the grizzly, Gunter's horse attempted to back up with only his hind legs on the ground. Monte nearly tipped over backward, which caused Gunter to lose his grip and fall off the horse, landing squarely on his back.

With the wind knocked out of him, unable to breathe for a few seconds, he gasped for air while attempting to shout as he scrambled instinctively to his feet. "Anya, get out of here!"

With her horse spinning in circles and kicking his back legs in the direction of the grizzly, Anya tried to shout back, "I got the spray, the bear spray."

"Throw it and leave," was all Gunter managed to say.

Struggling to free the can from the saddle bag while her horse was in constant motion made the task nearly impossible. The pressure on the reins was released momentarily, and in response, her horse took the cue and bolted off with Monte on his heels. Anya pulled back on the reins with all her might, but it was too late. Her horse was in full stride with his nose pushed away from his chest, making the hackamore useless. The bear spray remained in her saddle bag.

Play dead, echoed in Gunter's thoughts, but it seemed too late for that approach. This bear was on the attack. The bear, after all, had been provoked and was closing the space between itself and the one who invaded her territory.

The grizzly stood nearly seven feet as she pushed herself back onto her hind legs a second time. The throaty growl continued as it flashed its incisors. Gunter searched the ground for rocks to use as weapons. Not finding any, he considered attempting to use the side of the mountain as an escape route. Slowly he inched his way to the rim of the ridge. The drop-off was steep, and he thought if he could slide down, the bear might not follow. As he prepared to jump, the grizzly dropped to all fours and bounded in his direction.

Alice, Chuck, and Quad returned to camp earlier than expected, as the route they selected to reach the Continental Divide was more strenuous than Alice or Chuck were willing to endure.

Recuperating with trail mix and surveying the mountain ridge, they spotted two horses and riders traveling south to north, making their way along the Divide. They also noticed, some distance ahead of the riders, what they thought was a bear and a cub. Quad grabbed his binoculars and quickly determined that it was a grizzly sow with a cub. Moving the binoculars back and forth between the grizzly and the riders, he concluded that if the grizzly continued its current path, it would run directly into the riders.

Focusing on the riders, Quad said, "It's Gunter and Anya. I don't see Brit or her horse anywhere. This is not good. Something must be wrong."

As Alice inquired if there was any way to warn Gunter and Anya about the impending danger, Dusty, along with Bobby and Jack, rode into camp. Immediately upon dismounting, Dusty took charge.

"Jack, I am going to ask you to stay here in camp so Quad can use your horse. Bobby, are you willing to come along?"

"You bet."

"Quad, see if you can find a way to reach them directly."

"Boss," Quad's words nearly fell over themselves. Quad was not one to respond to a situation with panic, but the young cowboy couldn't spit the words out fast enough. Never lowering the binoculars, he said, "Someone's down off their horse, and the horses are running away. It must be Gunter because I can see Anya riding one of the horses."

Chuck joined the frantic conversation. "Can you see the bear? Is it on the ridge?"

"The bear is on the ridge, but I don't see Gunter."

Maintaining a level of calmness, Dusty issued directives. "Quad, look for the shortest route to the top of the ridge. Alice and Chuck, I need your help in collecting items I wish to take with us. Jack, when Shatz and Dillon return, have them bring the herd in and tie them to the line."

As though part of a chorus, the four answered, "Got it."

Having collected the items Dusty requested, Alice asked if there was anything else they could do.

Dusty stopped for a moment, looked directly at Alice, and said, "Yeah, pray."

"I already am.

The three guys headed out across the meadow and pushed their horses hard through the bog and up the side of the mountain as Quad had managed to find breaks in the trees where they were not forced to dismount. Once above the tree line, the push slowed as they, too, were forced to climb, creating their own switchbacks. Reaching the crest of the ridge, close to the spot where Quad saw Gunter's horse rear, they did not see the grizzly or her cub. They did see, however, coats covering a body, with Anya and Brit on each side of what was obviously Gunter.

Dusty, hoping for the best but prepared to encounter the worst, pulled two canvas wraps from the back of his horse and handed them to Bobby. "Once Anya has moved away from the body, you and Quad wrap it with these. There is rope in my saddle bags."

Taking a seat next to Anya, Dusty just sat. He didn't say anything because he knew there wasn't anything he could say. When she was ready, she would speak. He looked at Brit, whose face was washed in tears. All she could do was shake her head. Dusty closed his eyes and nodded, acknowledging he understood.

Startled to realize that she wasn't alone, Anya slowly lifted her head and stared at Dusty. Slowly, she allowed her body to tilt toward Dusty until she touched his shoulder, and then, like a flower, she wilted against him. He wrapped his arm around her and held her tight as she wept.

Some thirty minutes later, she sat upright and said, "We need to take him down from here, right?"

"Yeah, we do."

"What about Brit's horse? Do you know what happened to her horse?"

He looked at Quad, who nodded, signaling that he had spoken with Brit. "Don't worry, Quad will take care of it. Right now, I think we need to get up and moving around. You have been sitting for a long time."

"It all happened so fast. One minute we were talking, and the next. Oh, my god, he never heard the news."

"The news?" Dusty was confused by the redirection of the conversation.

"Oh, god. I was just about to tell him that he is going to be a grandpa."

Having safely returned to the campsite, Dusty informed Anya that he connected with Danelle and that she had notified the authorities. He also shared that the authorities were willing to fly a helicopter in to pick up Gunter. However, due to the changing weather pattern and the arrival of straight-line winds predicted to exceed eighty miles an hour, the window for such a flight was very narrow.

"Do we have to? Is there some sort of law that says his body must be flown out? If I have a say in the matter, I don't want that." She fought back tears as she continued to speak. "Dad always said, 'When my time comes, tie me to a horse and send me out into the wilderness.' If he had a choice, he would want to go out with the rest of us."

"The authorities can meet us tomorrow at our pickup site. I'll have Danelle make all the arrangements. It might not be what they want, but we'll deal with that when the time comes."

The evening meal was more about gathering as a group than consuming food. No one was hungry, but they couldn't encourage Anya to eat something if they didn't. The conversation, while staring at plates full of food, focused on how they successfully got Brit's horse down the mountain without damaging his leg any further.

Jack, a licensed farrier, inspected the leg the moment they returned to camp. Removing the wrap revealed that the cut, for the most part, hadn't done any serious damage. He concluded that the sole was more than likely bruised. "He's tender and probably will develop an abscess." Turning to Dusty, he said, "I can shoe him if you have any extra shoes, nails, and hammer, and that should get him home." He turned toward Brit and said, "The wrap was a good idea. It stopped the bleedin', kept the swellin' down, and I'm sure it added comfort to the horse. You did a good job wrapping it."

"Well, actually," she stopped herself, not sure if it was okay to use Gunter's name. Not knowing how else to say it, she said, "It was Gunter's idea, and it was Gunter who wrapped the leg."

"Of course, I should have known, the skill of a doctor."

Nervously, everyone looked at Anya, unsure how she would respond to hearing Gunter's name. Sensing their uncomfortableness, Anya looked up from her plate, still full of food, and said, "It's okay, everybody. I can't believe what happened. It hurts. But it would hurt even more if you all pretend it didn't happen or you avoid talking about Dad. I know I'm in shock, and it's going to take some time for it to all sink in, but—" There was a long pause before Anya finished. "But, I have to meet it head-on."

Shatz, who was seated closest to Anya, reached over and engulfed her with both arms and just held her. The embrace moved from seconds to minutes, and neither was inclined to speak. Sometimes the most powerful message is delivered without a single word spoken. Shatz slowly released Anya from her grasp and slid back to the center of the three-legged stool. Anya thanked her as she wiped the tears from her cheeks.

"Just tell us what you need. As I offered earlier, if it's okay with you, I'll sleep in your tent tonight."

"Thanks, Shatz. I would like that. But right now, I'm exhausted. I'm going to go lie down for a while. I will join you all later at the campfire."

Chuck, wanting to be helpful, quickly chimed in, "I'll walk you to your tent if you want."

"That's not necessary, but thank you, Chuck."

With Anya's departure, the rest of the group was able to process and express everything from confusion to grief. Together, they tried to determine exactly what unfolded on the Continental Divide between Gunter and the grizzly. Even though everyone realized it wouldn't change the outcome, there was a need to understand how such a horrible event could unfold.

They discussed how they could support Anya over the next twenty-four hours. It was also during this time that Dusty asked Bobby and Quad if they were comfortable placing Gunter's body in the mountain-fed stream that ran south of the campsite. The freezing water, Dusty suggested, would slow the decomposing process.

Both readily agreed and suggested that after the campfire, when Anya had turned in for the night, they move Gunter's body to the stream.

Even before darkness dropped over the meadow, the fire was burning. As usual, Jack functioned as the master architect of the fire. The structure was such that with a single match, the kindling at the base provided ample fuel to ensure that, eventually, the logs on the outer rim became a part of the fire. The design created its own draft that fed the fire during the initial stages.

Anya arrived at the campfire with Gunter's MP3 player in hand. She spoke without greeting anyone. "I have a song Dad shared with me the other night. I would like to play it for you all." Laughing to herself, she added, "I gave him this several years ago and didn't realize he ever figured out how to add music to a playlist." She paused for a moment as though she was watching him figure out how to work the contraption. Pulling her gaze away from the device, she continued, "I would also invite you all to share a glass of wine with me. Dad, as you may have noticed, liked his wine." As an afterthought, she quickly added, "If you don't drink, I understand."

With a glass of wine in everyone's hand, Anya took a seat next to the fire and pushed play. The meadow carried the music of two pianos accompanied by an orchestra across the bog and up to the trees. And then came the words that boomed forth, and Anya closed her eyes, and she saw Gunter everywhere. Each word of the song, in its own way, graced the far reaches of the Continental Divide, high above the group circling the fire. The refrain that followed echoed, in and around each soul, "*Fall on me ...*"

Chapter 11

The weather matched the mood in the camp. The clouds were thick and dark, so heavy that they appeared to be pressing down upon the earth. The wind raged forth in gusts and penetrated multiple layers of clothes. Even the thin tuft of hair on the horses' manes was under siege.

No one in camp slept, and therefore, everyone was up and moving about before the light from a darkened sun climbed the rim of the Continental Divide. Breakfast was a waste of preparation and food, as an appetite was nonexistent. Even the horses and mules mirrored the sober mood that pressed upon each person.

Jack and Bobby, who had spent each morning savoring a mug of coffee in the wilderness kitchen, couldn't force themselves to drink a drop, let alone sit on the three-legged stools.

By seven-thirty, more than an hour and a half ahead of schedule, the camp was packed in canvas bags and loaded upon the mules. The lone mule, the very mule who ponied behind Dusty's horse the entire trip, was given the task of carrying the most precious cargo. Gunter's body. The body was retrieved from the stream and carefully draped over the mule. The lone mule, shorter in stature than all the other mules, stood still as a rope secured the body to its back. Without a single word being uttered, Dusty softly lifted the reins, and his stout quarter horse stepped forth, and the mule fell into step and carried Gunter out of the big meadow beneath clouds that threatened to pour forth rain.

Anya placed her horse directly behind the mule and gave the gelding free rein. Surprisingly, despite the absence of pressure on his nose, he didn't try to lower his head and grab for grass. He simply marched on.

Unaware that the clouds could no longer hold the weight of the moisture, Anya, unlike the other riders, didn't reach for her slicker. Through the gift of prayer, she transcended the reality of the moment and entered a state of peace—a state where wetness couldn't bring harm to a person.

She couldn't remember the last time she prayed. It probably was as a child. Gunter would stroll into her room each night, stop at the bookshelf, and select a couple of children's books. With the final page read, the book was closed, and Gunter would ask what she was thankful for from the day. That would serve as the starting point of their evening prayers.

Without forethought, she heard Gunter's voice ask, "What are you thankful for?"

She began as she had as a young child. "I'm thankful for Mommy who gave me life, thankful for Daddy who protects my life." She abruptly stopped herself and started again. "I'm thankful for Mommy who gave me life, thankful for Daddy who protected my life. I'm thankful that together we rode the Continental Divide, thankful that he always asked me to fall on him, thankful that now he has fallen on me." The words rose like incense, an offering to God of thanks for the gift of Gunter.

Her horse's head pulled back as the lone mule wrung his tail, informing the gelding that he was getting too close to the cargo he was entrusted to carry. The sudden jolt awoke Anya from her prayer state, and she noticed the rain. Despite the driving force of each droplet, she turned her face toward the heavens and smiled. The wetness was God's grace raining down upon her and Gunter. It was God's invitation to fall on Him.

She turned and surveyed the caravan of riders that followed, and she smiled. Bobby, who was next in line, asked if everything was okay.

"Yes, Bobby. Everything is okay." She turned back and settled into the saddle, realizing that it would be a long day's ride.

The scenery, as Dusty had stated several times earlier in the week, was some of the most awesome, breathtaking sites imaginable. The landscape also resulted in some of the most strenuous and difficult riding, which was made more difficult because of the gale-force winds. The rain pulled back to a light mist as Dusty directed his horse off the trail and into the patch of green grass just beneath a waterfall. "We'll stop here for the morning break and wait for the mules to pass us. From here, we climb straight up and over the waterfalls. With this rain, the climb is going to be a challenge as the trail will be slick."

The climb was, as Dusty had predicted, challenging. A better word to describe the challenge was intense. The trail, never wider than two feet, was encased by trees. The center of which was washed out as a stream of water rushed downward. The horses were forced to straddle the washed-out middle of the trail while trying to dig into the red, slippery topsoil and leverage themselves upward. Switchbacks would have aided in the climb, but the density of the forest controlled the path.

Standing atop the waterfall, Dusty stopped his horse to give everyone a few minutes to relax the muscles of their lower back. For more than thirty minutes the riders had been leaning forward over their saddle to give their horse every advantage to climb the mountain. The muscles had been stretched and no doubt were rebelling. The stop also allowed Dusty, inconspicuously, to check the cargo atop the lone mule to ensure that it hadn't shifted.

The view before them was a maze of valleys and mountain peaks through which they would weave their way. Lifting the reins, signaling his horse to move out, Dusty informed everyone that for the next several hours, the wind would probably be even worse. And, as though on cue, the clouds pulled back their filter, and rain pummeled the group. Even the horses tilted their heads downward away from the rain.

The wind howled and pushed against their bodies. It was impossible to speak with one another as the wind captured the spoken word and cast it off before it reached another's ear. For the next two hours the group rode in silence and, whenever possible, tilted their heads upward to catch sight of beauty.

Heading toward what appeared to be a boxed-in canyon, the group encountered at black bear feeding on the edge of the trail. With the wind driving the smell and the sound of the group away from the bear, it didn't recognize that its lunch was being visited by uninvited guests. The moment the bear felt the ground shake, its head popped up, and it turned to face its unwelcome guests. Its first movement was away from the trail, but that exposed him as there was no cover. The bear stopped, turned, and raced back toward the trail, where he crossed directly in front of Dusty's horse and took off for the base of the valley that was thick with brush. In comparison to the grizzly, the black bear looked small, even though Dusty later commented, "That was one of the largest black bears I have seen in the Bob." It didn't matter the size or the color, a bear was a bear, and everyone's thoughts were back on the Continental Divide, with every eye on the lone mule's cargo.

It was Anya who broke the trance. "How long before we stop for lunch?"

Dusty pointed to the back end of the canyon and said, "Up ahead.

I'm hoping that the wind is not as bad or, at least, we can find some shelter next to the brush."

Dusty's hope was dashed as the wind didn't relent, and the brush offered minimal shelter. A drainage ditch provided some break to the wind, as long as one didn't drop down too far, as the bottom was flowing with water.

Despite the encouragement from Alice and Chuck, who sat with Anya, she didn't touch her sandwich. She agreed to try the trail mix, acknowledging that she needed to eat something, even though she didn't feel like it.

The three didn't say much as they sat with backs to the wind that, periodically, would whip down the embankment. From time to time, Chuck would attempt to offer some platitude of condolence, but before he could finish, Alice's hand rested heavily upon his thigh.

The only topic that garnered any length of conversation was the question, where do we go from here? All three offered options, but none felt confident with their selection.

When Dusty came to inform them that they would be moving out in fifteen minutes, Chuck asked, "Where do we go from here? The trail just seems to end up ahead."

Dusty gestured toward the bald-faced mountain directly across from them. "That there is known as Mount Patrick Gass. Notice a slight dip in the skyline of the mountain; that's the passage to the other side."

Staring at the treeless mountainside, Chuck commented, "But I don't see any trail."

"You will once we cross this stream farther down the trail and start the ascent. It is an endless series of switchbacks."

"Any idea the elevation of the pass?"

"It's a little shy of nine thousand feet. As I said, we will be moving on in about fifteen minutes. I'll have a few comments to share before we head down the trail."

Before everyone mounted, Dusty brought the group in close so they could hear him without having to yell. "Once we leave from here, we'll cross the stream and start climbing up Mount Patrick Gass. The mountain is named after Gass, who was a sergeant in the Lewis and Clark Expedition. He published the first journal of the adventure a year after the group returned. Our trip up the mountain today is going to be a bit of an expedition because the wind tends to swipe across the face of the mountain—one reason for the absence of trees. We may encounter a gust or two that could be quite forceful. Hold on to your horse and trust him. He will get you to the passage. Once we are on the other side, it shouldn't be as windy. We will follow the rim on the back side and then start our descent. The trail from there on out is good. We can walk if you want." Dusty paused, looked at Anya, and asked, "You are ready to continue?"

She nodded and stepped up into the saddle.

Scaling Mount Patrick Gass was every bit as challenging as Dusty predicted, and then some. At the first switchback, the clouds again couldn't hold back the moisture. A heavy mist, driven by the wind, fell sideways. The rocky trail became slippery, slowing the march upward even more.

Unlike the previous switchbacks, these were long straights of a gradual climb, followed by a switchback and then another long stretch in the opposite direction, followed by a switchback and then traveling back in the other direction.

In an effort to focus on something other than the danger of the moment, Anya began to count the switchbacks. At the sixth one, just as her horse was halfway through his turn, a mighty gust of wind lifted the horse and pushed him several feet up the trail. With her knuckles white from clinching the saddle horn, she was thankful that the wind drove the horse upward and not down. Lifting her head, she checked to make sure that Gunter's body was still atop the lone mule.

Nearing the top of Mount Patrick Gass, the sun, for a few seconds, broke through a small hole in the clouds. The sun's rays caught the mist particles and created a rainbow. Anya remembered the story Gunter told her as a young child, how God sent a rainbow as a sign to Noah that never again, never again. Anya breathed deeply and sat lightly in her saddle as she watched beneath the brim of her hat as Dusty skillfully ponied the lone mule. Gunter's body was never in danger.

Out of the wind, traveling the backside of the mountain, Anya softly started to sing to herself, "I Will Always Love You." Her voice grew, and soon the valley below carried forth each note, each word. Before her horse completed another stride, she heard music. She stopped singing for a moment and turned around to see Bobby accompanying her. Together they started again. Before long, the entire group was singing. Reaching the end of the final verse, everyone stopped singing and allowed Bobby and Anya to close out the song.

"*And I love you, will always love you.*"

Epilogue

One day short of five months after the funeral, Anya returned to the house in the country she once called home. Everything in the house was the same as the day Gunter left for Montana. The horse barn was a bit emptier, as all but two horses had been sold. The neighbor was taking care of them for the time being.

It was still difficult to believe that Jack, Bobby, and Dusty traveled all the way to Minnesota to attend Gunter's funeral. Equally surprising was Bobby, who made arrangements with the pastor to play "I Will Always Love You" on his mouth organ following the interment. Needless to say, there wasn't a dry eye in the crowd.

Anya still smiled every time she thought about the funeral. It was everything Gunter requested. Now, Anya had returned to the prairie of Minnesota for her daughter's baptism. The following day they would assemble at the baptismal font, the same font she was baptized at, the same font that stood next to Gunter's pine casket. The pastor cupped his hand, lifted water from the font, and poured it over Anya's daughter's head as he said, "Katharina Gunter Schaff, I baptize you in the name of the Father, and of the Son, and the Holy Spirit."

Following the church service, Anya drove back to the house, where she bundled up her daughter and took her down to see the horses. The first Sunday in February was exceptionally warm, so she decided to take advantage of the weather.

The two horses greeted them at the gate and stretched their noses toward Anya and Katharina, waiting to be stroked. As Anya stood with one hand on a horse and another holding her daughter, it felt right. It felt like a place to raise a daughter. It felt like a place where the divide that once separated a father from his daughter and a daughter from her father had been conquered.

At that moment, she needed to say out loud, "Dad, we're home! Katharina Gunter, welcome to your new home. May you ride through life as well as your grandpa did!"

Katharina, worn out from the long morning, fell against her mommy's chest. Anya whispered softly to her daughter, "Fall on me, fall on me."

Acknowledgements

The creation and publication of a book is *never* a one-person enterprise. Successful authors surround themselves with a legion of people who will challenge them, critique their work, and support them through the entire process. *Fall On Me* began as a seed of an idea when my daughter Anikka accepted my invitation to ride the Continental Divide. The seed germinated during the 10-day trip. The excitement from fellow riders who were intrigued by the rough plot outline provided the incentive to make the trip a working trip. I need to express a sincere word of gratitude to the 7 Lazy P Guest Ranch. Dusty and Michelle are amazing hosts.

Dusty—Anikka captured you well after the trip, "From now on when I think of a cowboy, I will see you. You knew when to use your voice and when to be silent."

I also wish to thank the wranglers and my fellow riders for making the trip enjoyable. Without all of you, there would not be a book.

A month after returning home, I finished writing the book. I sent a copy to Shannon Ishizaki, the owner of Orange Hat Publishing. The support and demand for quality work begins with Shannon Ishizaki and is put into practice with the staff. I cannot imagine ever working with another publishing company. Orange Hat Publishing | Ten16

Press strives to put forth quality books while supporting the authors through the entire process.

Without the critical eye of proofreader Shannon Booth, readers of this book would need to wade through a plethora of commas. Shannon—Thank you for cleaning up the manuscript.

Thank you to Michael Braun, who managed this project and is now the new owner of Orange Hat Publishing. Michael—You went above and beyond to work through the logistical issues and ensure that the manuscript was ready for publication.

Anikka—Thank you for your willingness to accompany me on this adventure. Thank you for sharing your artistic abilities in providing a sketch for each chapter. There would not be a book if you had not sat atop a horse for ten days.

Tammie, my soulmate—Thank you for staying home and taking care of the horses and dogs so that I might add a checkmark to my bucket list.

Finally, readers—Thank you for riding along with us and crossing the Continental Divide. I invite you to check out my other books and look for *The Soul of The Shoe* soon to be released by Orange Hat Publishing | Ten16 Press.

Happy Trails!

Douglas Knick's professional career includes ordained ministry, an associate professor at Luther College, and a high school social studies teacher. He is the co-founder and director of Delta Equine Center, providing educational opportunities, horse training, and equine bodywork. Since retiring, he has had more time to focus on his writing and his life's passion for working with and learning from horses. Doug lives in Spicer, MN, with his wife, Tammie Haven Knick, two Australian Shepherds, and five horses.